THE HOWLING
MILLER

Other books by Arto Paasilinna published in English

The Year of the Hare

THE HOWLING MILLER

Arto Paasilinna

Translated by Will Hobson
from the French of Anne Colin du Terrail

CANONGATE

Edinburgh · New York · Melbourne

Originally published in Finland in 1981 as *Ulvovo mylläri* by WSOY

First English translation published in Great Britain in 2007 by Canongate Books, Ltd Edinburgh

Printed in the United States of America
Published simultaneously in Canada

FIRST AMERICAN EDITION

ISBN-10: 1-84767-181-0

ISBN-13: 978-1-84767-181-3

Canongate
841 Broadway
New York, NY 10003

Distributed by Publishers Group West

www.groveatlantic.com

08 09 10 11 12   10 9 8 7 6 5 4 3 2 1

PART ONE

The madman's mill

CHAPTER 1

Soon after the wars, a tall fellow appeared in the canton who said his name was Gunnar Huttunen. Unlike most of the drifters who came up from the south, he didn't go to the forestry department looking for work digging ditches, but bought the old mill on the Suukoski rapids of the Kemijoki River. This was judged to be a hare-brained scheme, since, having stood idle since the 1930s, the mill had fallen into a state of extreme dilapidation.

Be that as it may, Huttunen paid the asking price and moved into the mill house. The local farmers and, in particular, the members of the Suukoski Millers' Cooperative laughed until tears filled their eyes at the news of the sale. Apparently the world's not short of fools, they observed to one another, even though the wars killed off a good few.

That first summer Huttunen repaired the shingle saw

at the mill. He put an advertisement in the *Northern News* offering a reliable splitting service, and from then on, all the canton's barns were roofed with wooden tiles split at the Suukoski mill. Huttunen's shingles worked out six times cheaper than the factory-made asphalted felt, which, anyway, had been hard to come by since the Germans had burnt Lapland to the ground and building materials of all kinds had grown terribly scarce. Sometimes you had to hand over anything up to twelve pounds of butter at the village shop before you could load a single roll of roofing felt onto your cart. The shopkeeper Tervola knew better than anyone the going rate of his wares.

Gunnar Huttunen was almost six feet three inches tall. He had straight brown hair and bony features: a jutting chin, long nose, and deep-set eyes under a flat, high forehead. His cheekbones were prominent, his face narrow. His ears, although big, did not stick out, but lay flush against his skull. It was obvious that, as a baby, a careful eye had been kept on the sleeping Gunnar Huttunen. If a child has big ears, you must never allow it to roll over by itself in its cot; mothers must turn little boys over from time to time if they don't want them growing up to be lop-eared men.

As lean as he was tall, Gunnar Huttunen carried himself very erect. When he walked, he took a stride at least one and a half times that of most men's; in the snow, his footprints looked like those of an average-sized person running. At the first snowfall, he split himself a pair of skis that were long enough to touch the eaves of an ordinary house. In these, he laid broad, pretty much straight tracks and, being light, he tended to plant the poles to the same steady rhythm. You always knew immediately from the pole marks if Huttunen had been by.

No one was ever too sure exactly where he was from originally. Some said Ilmajoki, whereas others happened to know for a fact that he had come to Lapland from Satakunta. Or Laitila. Or Kiikoiset. When someone asked him once why he had moved up north, the miller had said his mill in southern Finland had burnt down. He had lost his wife in the same fire. His insurance hadn't compensated him for either.

'They went up in flames together,' Gunnar Huttunen said, giving his questioner a strangely chilling look. After raking up his wife's bones from the blackened wreckage of the mill and laying them to rest in the churchyard, Huttunen had sold the rubble and land that was now abhorrent to him, relinquished his water rights, and left the area for good. He said it had been his good fortune to find a decent mill up here in the north and, although it wasn't working yet, the income from the shingle saw was enough for a single man to live on.

The one problem, however, as the municipal clerk made sure everyone knew, was that according to the parish records the miller Gunnar Huttunen was a bachelor. So how could he have lost a wife in a fire? This proved the subject of much debate. But no one ever discovered the truth about the miller's past and in the end people lost interest. They simply figured that it can't have been the

5

first time someone's wife had burnt, or been burnt, to death down there in the south, and they didn't seem to be in noticeably short supply.

Gunnar Huttunen periodically suffered long bouts of depression. He would break off in the middle of whatever he was doing and stare into the distance, apparently aimlessly. Anguish glinted in the depths of his dark eyes; they became probing and caustic, and yet full of melancholy. If he caught your eye, the brilliant glitter of his stare would make you shudder, and anyone talking to Huttunen during one of his black moods would be hit by a wave of sadness and dismay.

But the miller wasn't always low, by any stretch of the imagination. He often kicked up a tremendous ruckus for no obvious reason. He'd get up to all sorts of high jinks, joking and laughing, and sometimes cast aside all restraint to caper about on his long legs in the most comical fashion. Holding forth on this or that, he'd gesticulate wildly, cracking his knuckles, waving his arms and craning his neck as he held forth on this or that. He'd come out with incredible cock and bull stories, blithely getting people worked up just for the fun of it, or he'd slap a farmer on the back, shower him with unwarranted praise, laugh in his face, and then wink at the fellow and clap his hands.

When Huttunen was having one of these good spells, all the young people in the village would gather at Suukoski to watch the miller's exuberant performances. They'd crowd into the ground floor of the mill, just like in the old days, and tell each other jokes and stories. In the peaceful, cheery gloom, amid the dark, heady smells of the old mill, everyone would be happy and full of high spirits. Sometimes Gunnar – or Kunnari, as they called him in the Finnish way – would light a big fire outside, and they'd feed it with dry shingles and grill whitefish from the Kemijoki.

The miller had a great gift for imitating the animals of the forest. He would make a game of it, and the youngsters would compete to see who could be the first to guess which animal he was mimicking. One minute he would become a hare, and then the next a lemming or a bear. Sometimes he would flap his long arms like a night owl, or start howling like a wolf, pointing his nose at the sky and letting out such a heart-rending wail that the terrified youngsters would huddle together for comfort.

He often did impressions of the canton's farmers and farmwives as well, which his audiences would be equally quick to guess. When the miller transformed himself into a short, stout character which required a great deal of concentration on his part, everyone would know without a moment's hesitation that he was imitating his nearest neighbour, fat Vittavaara.

Those were extraordinary summer evenings and nights, but people sometimes had to look forward to them for weeks on end while Gunnar Huttunen remained sunk in silent gloom. If that were the case, then no one from the village would dare go to the mill unless they had business there and everyone would try to conclude their

7

transactions as quickly as possible, with the minimum of conversation, so daunted were they by the miller's misery.

As time passed, Huttunen's attacks of depression seemed to grow more acute. He was abrasive, shouting at people for no reason, and seemed permanently on edge. Occasionally he would be so overwrought and furious that he would refuse to give farmers the shingles they had ordered, and just snarl, 'Can't help. They're not ready.' Then there was nothing for the buyer to do but leave empty-handed, even if several steres of freshly cut shingle were there for all to see, neatly piled up next to the bridge.

When his mood lifted, however, Huttunen was even more peerless than ever. He performed like a circus ring-master, his wit as sharp as the gleaming blade of the shingle saw. His movements were so quick and supple, his impressions so ebullient and startling that his audiences were utterly bewitched. Until the inevitable moment when, at the peak of his merrymaking, the miller would suddenly freeze; a harsh cry would burst from his lips and then he would be off, running out of sight behind the mill, along the rotten millrace, across the river and into the forest. He would plunge blindly through the trees, branches snapping and whistling behind him, and when he arrived back at the mill an hour or two later, tired and out of breath, the youngsters of the village would slip away home and announce in frightened voices that Kunnari's bad days had returned.

People began to think Gunnar Huttunen was mad.

His neighbours told stories in the village of the way

Kunnari had of howling like a wild animal, especially on clear winter nights when there was a hard frost. He would howl from dusk until the early hours and, if it were carried on the wind, every dog for miles around would answer his desolate outcry. All the villages along the great river lay awake on those nights and people would say that poor Kunnari really must be wrong in the head to think of getting the dogs worked up at such a godforsaken hour.

'Someone should go and tell him to stop howling, a man his age. A human being can't just start baying like a bloody wolf.'

But no one dared bring up the matter with Huttunen. His neighbours told themselves that maybe he would come to his senses at some point and stop of his own accord.

'Let him howl, you get used to it in the long run,' declared the farmers, who needed shingles. 'He's crazy, but he splits good tiles and they're reasonably priced.'

'He's promised to get the mill working, so we'd best not upset him, otherwise he might move back down south,' said other farmers, who planned to plant wheat on the banks of the Kemijoki.

CHAPTER 2

One spring when the thaw came, the river rose so high that Gunnar Huttunen almost lost his mill. Under the weight of floodwater, the dam at the head of the millrace gave way across a two-yard stretch. Thick sheets of ice surged through the gap. They smashed up fifteen yards of the dilapidated channel, broke the wheel of the shingle saw, and would have brought down the whole mill if Huttunen hadn't rushed to its rescue. He ran to the saw's sluice gate and wrenched it open, steering the mass of water out through the broken wheel into the lower reaches of the river. But all the while floodwater continued to pour through the broken dam, driving huge drifts of ice before it that piled up against the mill wall, until the old wooden building began to tremble under their weight. Huttunen was afraid the mill would break apart and the heavy millstones fall through the floor onto the turbine and smash that too. At this point he had no choice but to jump on his bicycle and pedal to the village shop nearly one and a half miles away.

Breathless and pouring with sweat, Huttunen yelled at the shopkeeper Tervola, who was measuring grain, 'Give me some stump bombs! Now!'

The sudden appearance of the miller, drenched in sweat and demanding explosives, scared the life out of a handful of village gossips who were doing their shopping. From behind his scales, Tervola began to ask Huttunen for his licence for the purchase and possession of explosives but when the miller bellowed that the ice would destroy the whole Suukoski mill if it weren't blasted, in a panic the shopkeeper sold him a case of stump bombs, a spool of fuse and a handful of detonators. These were packed up in a cardboard box, which Huttunen strapped to his bicycle rack, and then he leapt into the saddle and rode at top speed back to the Suukoski rapids where the river was still rising and the ice smashing into the rickety pilings of the old mill. Tervola instantly shut up shop and, with the old biddies in tow, hurried off to see how Huttunen would manage. But not before taking time to call the entire village. 'Come out to Suukoski if you want to see Huttunen's mill fall into the river,' he shouted down the telephone.

An explosion could soon be heard echoing up from Suukoski. As the people from the shop and the rest of the village came rushing up to take their places on the bank, another blast followed. Shattered ice and chunks of wood flew into the air. The children were forbidden to go too near the water. A few farmers who'd just arrived called out to Huttunen asking him what they should do; they wanted to help.

But Huttunen was so frantic and busy that he didn't have time to give instructions. Grabbing a saw and an axe, he ran along the edge of the millrace to the dam, jumped over the banked-up ice into the river, waded through the thigh-deep water and, like a woodcutter, began sizing up a dense stand of spruce on the opposite bank.

'Kunnari's in such a hurry, he hasn't even got time to howl,' said the fat-bellied Vittavaara.

'No time for elk or bear imitations, though he's got the audience for it,' someone else said, to general laughter.

But Constable Portimo, a peaceable old man, told them to be quiet.

'You don't make fun of a man when he's in trouble.'

Huttunen chose a tall spruce by the water's edge. Striking it a few firm blows with his axe, he lined up its fall with a point directly across the river. Then he bent down and began sawing. The crowd of spectators on the other bank wondered why on earth the miller had suddenly started tree felling. Was there something more important than saving the mill? A farmhand called Launola who had hurried up from the village said, 'He's completely forgotten about the mill and just thought he'd cut a nice bit of timber!'

Huttunen heard this comment from the other bank. He flushed angrily, the blood pounding in his temples,

13

and almost stood up and shouted something back at the farmhand, but in the end simply kept on sawing at furious speed.

The giant spruce soon began to teeter. Pulling his saw out of the split, Huttunen jemmied the massive trunk with the blade of his axe until it gave, and, with its great canopy of spreading branches, the tree plunged into the flooded river, smashing through the ice piled up against the dam. A murmur ran through the crowd of villagers. Now they understood. The tree glided downstream and docked alongside the dam, forming a barrier to the drift ice swept along by the rapids: the floodwaters could still skirl freely between its tangle of branches into the broken millrace, but the ice could no longer get through and so the danger had been averted.

Gunnar Huttunen wiped the sweat from his face, crossed the river by the bridge, walked into the mill and emerged the other side before his waiting audience. 'There, just thought I'd cut a nice bit of timber,' he growled at Launola, the farmhand.

The crowd stirred irritably. The men said they were sorry not to have had time to help the miller. 'That was good thinking, Kunnari,' they said, congratulating him on felling the tree into the river.

The excitement was over, but the villagers didn't seem able to leave. The opposite, in fact: others were still trickling in from the village, with the corpulent Mrs Siponen bringing up the rear, breathlessly asking if she had missed much.

Huttunen primed another stump bomb and demanded loudly, 'Did the show seem too short? Well, let's give you some more, then. We wouldn't want such a big crowd to have come all this way for nothing, would we.'

The miller began to do an imitation of a crane. He hopped up onto the edge of the millrace, gave a loud trumpet, and then bent down and stretched out his neck as if he were looking for frogs in the water.

Disgruntled, Huttunen's audience prepared to leave the riverbank. People tried to calm the miller down. 'He's really crazy,' someone groaned. Amid the to-ing and fro-ing, Huttunen lit the stump bomb; its fuse began hissing viciously. There was a general stampede. The villagers took to their heels, but many had still only gone a few paces when Huttunen threw the charge into the river, where it instantly exploded. With a dull boom, the bomb showered the bank with water and shards of ice, soaking the crowd. They fled screaming and did not stop until they had reached the road, from where they hurled a stream of furious abuse back at the Suukoski mill.

CHAPTER 3

When the river subsided, Gunnar Huttunen set about repairing the damage to the mill. He ordered three cart-loads of timber from the sawmill: beams, planks and boards. He bought two cases of nails from Tervola, one of hobnails, the other of four-inch nails. He hired three out-of-work farmhands from the village to drive new piles for the broken dam. Within a few days, the dam was repaired and the sluice gate could once again harness the river's power. Huttunen sent the farmhands home and turned his attention to the millrace. He completely rebuilt the section between the dam and the wheel of the shingle saw; this alone required one and a half cartloads of five-inch planks.

Those were beautiful summer days, with a perfect, mild breeze, and the miller was in excellent spirits. Huttunen was good with his hands and liked this sort of carpenter's work. He got so caught up in the repairs that he barely took the time to sleep. He would hurry out to the mill-race at four or five in the morning, cut planks and beams until daybreak, go inside to brew some coffee and then go straight back out to work. In the hottest part of the day, he would lie down for an hour or two in the mill house, and often falling asleep and waking up refreshed and full of energy in the late afternoon. Then he would have something to eat and rush back out to the millrace. You could hear the heavy thud of axe and hammer from the Suukoski mill until late into the night.

People began to say Kunnari was twice as mad as most people: he behaved like a maniac, for a start, and now it seemed he worked like one too.

After a week and a half, the millrace was fixed and tightly sealed throughout. It fed the river water down from the dam to where it was needed to drive the mill and the shingle saw. Huttunen moved onto the saw wheel. All the paddles were rotten through and had to be replaced. But the axle was still in a decent state, he saw. If he just replaced the spindle on one side and the sleeve, it would work fine.

This done, the miller stripped to his underwear and waded out into the river to reinstall the wheel. And it was at that moment that the mill received a visit.

A woman appeared on the mill bridge. She was thirty or so, Junoesque and rosy-cheeked, radiant in a flowery summer dress and a brightly coloured scarf. She was beautiful, bursting with life and vigour, but her voice was as delicate as a little girl's, and Huttunen didn't hear her over the roar of the rapids when she shouted, 'Mr Huttunen! Mr Huttunen!'

The woman watched the almost naked man set about his task. Struggling with all his might against the cold water, the lean, wiry miller fought to wrestle the wheel into place, but the spindle kept on coming off the axle, the current was too strong. At last, with a supreme effort, he managed to force the huge wheel home. He set it free, the paddles filled with water and it began turning at once, slowly at first, and then faster. Stepping back to observe his handiwork, Huttunen declared, 'Got you, you bastard.'

Once the flow of water had been channelled, the miller heard a clear woman's voice calling, 'Mr Huttunen!'

He turned towards the sound. A young woman stood on the bridge. She had taken off her scarf and was waving it in a very fetching way, freeing her blonde, natural curls. She looked gorgeous, silhouetted there in the sunshine and summer breeze. As he gazed up at her from the river, Huttunen noticed her powerful thighs and sturdy calves. When the wind lifted her dress, he could even see her underwear – seamed stockings and garters alike. She didn't seem to realise she presented such an edifying prospect, or perhaps wasn't embarrassed about showing a glimpse of her thighs. Huttunen hauled himself out of the river, grabbed his clothes from the bridge and quickly got dressed. The woman walked over to the mill, and then turned and offered the miller her hand.

'I'm the 4H adviser,* Sanelma Käyrämö.'

'Pleased to meet you,' Huttunen managed to reply.

'I'm the association's new horticulture adviser here. I'm visiting all the households in the district, even those without any young people. I've already visited sixty, but I've still got a long way to go.'

Horticulture adviser? What business could someone from the 4H Federation have at the mill?

'Your neighbour Mrs Vittavaara told me you lived here on your own,' Sanelma Käyrämö continued, 'and I decided to come and see you. A bachelor can grow vegetables too, after all.'

Whereupon, the horticulture adviser launched into an enthusiastic exposition of her field of expertise. Growing vegetables was the best thing in the world you could do if you lived in the country: they were an excellent additional source of food, and provided a wonderful balance of vitamins and mineral salts. A vegetable garden of just half an acre could keep a small family hale and hearty for an entire winter – provided it was properly looked after, of course. It was all just a matter of rolling up one's sleeves and getting stuck in. She couldn't tell him how rewarding it was!

'So, Mr Huttunen, don't you think we should start planning a lovely vegetable garden for you? Vegetables

* A rural youth educational organisation, the 4H Federation teaches practical skills to young people in rural areas – courses range from animal husbandry and horticulture to home economics and computing – and encourages enterprise and self-reliance. It is named after 'the four Hs': Head, Hands, Heart and Health – Harkinta, Harjaanus, Hyvyys, Hyvinvointi in Finnish. It was established in the USA in the early 1900s, and has branches in eighty countries.

are so fashionable nowadays that even a man needn't be embarrassed about growing or eating them.'

Huttunen started to protest. Living alone, he said, he was quite happy buying the odd sack of turnips or swede from his neighbours when the need arose.

'Say no more!' Sanelma Käyrämö broke in. 'We're going to get the ball rolling right away. I'll give you some seeds to get started. Now let's go and see if we can find a suitable spot for your garden. I've never known anyone who was sorry they took up growing vegetables.'

Huttunen made another attempt to deter her.

'But the thing is, I'm a . . . a bit crazy. Didn't they tell you in the village, Miss?'

The horticulture adviser brushed aside Huttunen's mental instability with a casual wave of her scarf as if she had been dealing with the disturbed all her life. She took the miller firmly by the hand and led him to the mill yard. There she sketched out the dimensions of his garden-to-be in the air. The miller's head spun as he followed her sweeping gestures; the veg patch seemed enormous. He grimaced, she scaled it down a little, and then that appeared to be that. The matter was settled. She broke off four birch branches and stuck them in the ground at each of the corners.

'It has to be a garden this size for a man as tall as you,' she said, before going to fetch her briefcase from her bicycle. She sat down on the grass, opened the briefcase and took out a sheaf of papers that she spread on the ground. The wind caught a few and blew them away;

21

Huttunen went and fetched them from the riverbank, not quite able to believe what was happening; it all seemed marvellous to him. When he handed the papers back to the adviser she thanked him with an adorable laugh. This made him so happy he felt like howling with delight, and almost did so, but then restrained himself. He thought it was better to behave normally in front of a woman like this, at least at first.

The adviser signed up the miller Gunnar Huttunen as a member of the local 4H Club. She drew a plan of the vegetable garden and wrote on it what he should grow: beetroot, carrots, turnips, peas, onions and herbs. She added spring cabbage, but then crossed it out because there weren't any in the village.

'It'll probably be better, for our first season, if we stick to the most common varieties. Then, after we've had a little practice, we can increase our repertoire,' she decided. She gave Huttunen several packets of seeds, saying she'd collect the money for them on her next visit.

'We have to see if they come up first . . . But I'm quite sure, Mr Huttunen, that you will soon be witnessing the miracle of life and growth.'

Huttunen was doubtful about his ability to tend the garden; he said he had never done anything like it before. Such hesitancy did not even merit discussion, as far as the horticulture adviser was concerned, however, and she began explaining how to grow the vegetables and giving the miller detailed instructions on how to work and fertilise the soil, how to start the seeds, how deeply to plant them, and what were the ideal spacings between different species. Vegetable gardening soon struck Huttunen as not just extraordinarily fascinating but also ideal for him since there wouldn't be enough work at the mill to keep him busy all summer. He told the horticulture adviser he'd get started right away and hurried off to get a shovel and a hoe from the shed.

Sanelma Käyrämö watched the tall man drive his hoe into the ground. The blade tore up big clumps of earth that the miller then turned over. She bent down to pick up some soil, rubbed it between her fingers, sniffed it and said it would be impossible to find a better spot for a vegetable garden. Seeing the adviser had got her hand dirty, Huttunen dashed into the mill to fetch a zinc bucket, splashed into the river to fill it and brought it back to her so she could wash her fingers.

'Oh, you shouldn't have,' said the horticulture adviser, blushing, as she rinsed her fingers in the bucket. 'Your trousers are wet up to the knee. How can I make it up to you?'

Who cares about trousers, Huttunen thought happily. The adviser was pleased, that was the main thing. He set to hoeing again with such a will that an ox and plough would have been hard pressed to keep up.

The horticulture adviser put her papers back in her briefcase, fetched her bicycle and put out her hand in farewell.

'If any problems crop up, do get in touch,' she urged. 'I live upstairs at the Siponens'. Don't be shy. You're a beginner and I may easily have forgotten to explain something.'

Then she knotted her brightly coloured scarf over her blonde curls, hooked her briefcase over her handlebars and got onto her bicycle, her ample bottom entirely enveloping its seat. Her light dress fluttered in the wind as she rode away.

When she got to the woods, she stopped her bicycle and turned to look at the mill, sighing, 'My goodness . . .'

In a state of high excitement, Huttunen didn't know what to do after the adviser had left. Hoeing the garden had lost some of its urgency. He strode restlessly into the mill, leant against the millstone, rubbed his hands and closed his eyes, thinking of her. Suddenly his whole body tensed and he dashed outside. He ran under the millrace and into the river, plunging into the cool water up to his neck. When he climbed out, he was shivering a little but he felt calmer. He went into the mill, looked out of the little window at the road and whined quietly, but didn't howl as he did in winter.

Huttunen finished digging the garden that evening and spread a load of manure after night had fallen. He raked the manure into the soil and sowed the seeds the horticulture adviser had given him. It wasn't until after midnight that he finished watering his patch and finally went to bed.

Huttunen drifted off to sleep a happy man. He now had his very own vegetable garden. And that meant that the lovely 4H adviser would soon be riding out to see him again.

CHAPTER 4

Huttunen continued repairing the flood damage over the following days. He overhauled the chute between the mill and the shingle saw, which, in places, only required replacing a plank or two. He added new beams under the millrace. Many of the old ones were rotten. When he got up on the edge of the channel and bounced up and down, it swayed precariously and shipped water, which reduced the flow and the power the wheel could generate.

After five days' work, Huttunen was ready to test the mill. He closed the sluice gate to the saw wheel to steer all the water into the turbine house. The turbine began turning, lethargically at first, and then faster and faster. After checking it was rotating evenly and that there was an adequate water flow, Huttunen climbed up onto the bridge from the turbine house and went into the mill. He greased the main axles and bearings and, using an oilcan with a long spout, dabbed machine oil into every working part. He took an aspen spatula and applied belt resin to the pull-wheel of the turbine axle; the stuff spread easily if he pressed the tool hard against the turning drum. He rubbed resin on the gears that drove the shaft of the upper millstone, the runner stone, and then ran the driving belt round the drum, giving it a twist to keep it in place. Moving to the snaking rhythm of the turbine axle, the wide belt set the heavy runner stone turning, and it began to grind against the motionless bedstone beneath it. Had Huttunen poured a few handfuls of grain into the eye, a smell of flour would soon have drifted up into the air.

The mill was working. The stones turned with a muffled roar, the driving belt gripped, the axles clattered in their gleaming housings and the whole building shook, while down below the millstream seethed in the turbine house.

Huttunen tested the millstones methodically, switching the driving belt from the ones for flour to the ones for animal feed, and then the huller wheel. They all worked fine too.

The miller sat down on the edge of the empty grain bin, closed his eyes and listened to the familiar sounds of the mill. His face relaxed, showing no trace of either his customary elation or despondency. He let the mill run empty for a long time before diverting the water away from the turbine. The wheel gradually stopped turning and came to a complete halt. The mill was silent again, the only sound the gentle babble of the river as it slipped beneath the building.

The following morning, Huttunen went to the shop to announce that, should anyone need any of last year's fodder ground, he was ready to start milling.

The shopkeeper Tervola greeted him with a sideways look. 'I had to put those stump bombs in my name when the police asked me if you had a licence. I'm not selling you any more explosives without a licence. You're too odd.'

Huttunen walked around the shop as if he hadn't heard the reproach. He fished a bottle of pilsner out of a crate and lit a cigarette. It was his last one, conveniently enough. He tore the back off the cigarette packet and wrote a notice to the effect that the Suukoski mill was back in operation and people could take their grain there to be milled. Then he took an old drawing pin from the shop door and stuck up his announcement.

'Why did you blow up that charge in the river when all those people were on the bank?' asked Tervola, as he weighed out some mixed dried fruit for the schoolteacher's wife. Huttunen put the empty beer bottle back in its crate and tossed a couple of coins onto the counter. The shopkeeper leant over his scales and continued grumbling.

'The council said you ought to be put away somewhere where you can have your head examined.'

Huttunen abruptly swung round towards the shopkeeper and, looking him straight in the eye, asked, 'Tell me, Tervola, why do you think my carrots haven't come up yet? I've watered them every day until the soil's black, but not a glimmer.'

The shopkeeper muttered that nobody had said anything about carrots. 'This is the second summer my daughter's been hanging around your mill. Are we supposed to let our children stay out all night, and listen to a lunatic while they're at it?'

Huttunen put his fist on the scales and pushed down.

'Twenty pounds exactly. Put another weight on.'

Huttunen added some weights to the scales himself, and then pressed down again.

'Now my hand weighs thirty pounds.'

The shopkeeper tried to get Huttunen's fist off the scales. The bag of mixed fruit was knocked over in the tussle, dried apple scattering across the floor. The schoolteacher's wife backed away from the counter.

Suddenly Huttunen gathered up the scales in his arms and walked out of the shop, tearing his notice off the door with his teeth on the way. In the yard outside, he put the scales in the bucket of the draw well and then carefully lowered it to the bottom. Tervola stormed out after him, shouting from the top of the steps that Huttunen had played his last prank.

'You belong in a padded cell! The sooner the better! You're barred from this shop from now on, Huttunen!'

The miller headed towards the church, wondering how it had come to this. He felt downcast, but the thought of the scales at the bottom of the draw well cheered him up. A draw well is a sort of scale, anyway. Just one that uses water instead of weights.

When he got to the churchyard, Huttunen stopped and, using one of the assortment of old nails from previous notices, stuck the back of the cigarette packet he had been carrying in his teeth on the gatepost. His announcement read:

Suukoski mill is turning again.
Huttunen

From the churchyard, Huttunen walked to the café by the church. He ordered a bottle of pilsner and, as the place was full of idlers from all parts of the canton, he stood up and announced, 'Put the word out that anyone who's still got grain can take it to Suukoski.'

He finished his beer and, on his way out, added at the door, 'But no treated grain. I won't mill it, even if it's for fodder. It fouls up the stones.'

The miller slowed as he reached the Siponens' farm, scanning the upstairs windows to see if the horticulture adviser was at home. He looked for her blue bicycle, but he couldn't see it. She must be doing the rounds of the villages, teaching children how to look after vegetables and swapping vegetable recipes with farmers' wives. Huttunen felt jealous at the thought of her at that moment initiating some tongue-tied, snotty-nosed youngster into the art of thinning carrots, or advising some plump farmwife on how to chop lettuce leaves. Huttunen thought of his own, heavily watered vegetable patch. So, the adviser didn't have time to come and visit, was that it? She could have at least dropped by to see how faithfully he had hoed and fertilised and planted his garden. He'd followed her every instruction to the letter.

Had she been making fun of him, persuading a grown man to do a child's work? Everyone in the canton laughed at him as it was, 'the crazy beanpole'. Had she joined the chorus? The thought was an unbearably sad and painful one to Gunnar Huttunen. He turned his back on the Siponen house and ran feverishly back to Suukoski.

He encountered the schoolteacher's wife on her way back from the shop. When she saw Huttunen tearing down the road, she stopped her bicycle and let him sweep in front of her into the woods.

Huttunen stopped in the mill yard to inspect his vegetable garden. It lay there, black and lifeless. He studied the soil with its air of neglect, and felt equally abandoned by the horticulture adviser. Climbing sadly up to his little room at the top of the mill, he kicked off his Wellington boots and threw himself on his bed without having anything to eat. He lay there sighing heavily for two hours, and then fell into a fitful sleep, haunted by confused, disturbing dreams.

CHAPTER 5

When the miller woke up early the next morning and consulted his pocket watch, it said four o'clock. It was a superb watch. He had bought it between the wars from a penniless German sergeant passing through Riihimäki, who had sworn it was as waterproof as it was accurate. Over the years, this claim had been proved correct. Huttunen had once bet a group of forestry workers that his timepiece could take anything. He had put it in his mouth, settled down in a sauna for over an hour, and then dived into a lake twice. He had swum to the bottom and lain there not moving, listening to the ticking of the second hand that, thanks to the water pressure, echoed through his skull as clear as a bell. When he spat out the watch after the experiment and dried it, it was working as well as if it had remained snug in his pocket all along. The parts hadn't suffered in the slightest. So. It was definitely four o'clock.

After winding up the watch, Huttunen thought about the horticulture adviser. He remembered her saying that if he had the slightest problem with his vegetable patch, he shouldn't hesitate to go and talk to her about it.

What if he went to see her now to discuss the garden? Huttunen felt he had reason enough to pay her a visit: it was six days since he'd planted the seeds she'd given him and they'd shown absolutely no signs of life. He could find out whether the seeds were last year's or, if it came to that, ask her if she had any better ones. Turning the matter over in his mind, Huttunen came to the conclusion that he clearly had no shortage of important – official, virtually – matters to discuss with the adviser. No one could possibly criticise him if he went and paid her a visit now.

He drank half a ladle of cold water and set off on his bicycle for the Siponens' farm.

The village was strangely deserted: no cattle in the pastures, no one working in the fields. Only the birds were singing, already woken by the summer dawn, and a few sleepy dogs barked lazily as the miller rode past. No smoke rose from any of the chimneys; everyone was still in bed.

The Siponens' dog began barking ferociously as Huttunen rode his bicycle into the farmyard. The front door was off the latch and Huttunen walked into the parlour where the curtains were drawn and everyone was asleep.

'Morning.'

The farmhand Launola was the first member of the

household to wake up; drowsy and amazed, he returned the miller's greeting from his bunk on the other side of the stove. Then the head of the house emerged from his room, a small, short-sighted old man who looked like an elephant. He walked over to Huttunen, peered up at his face, realised who it was and invited him to sit down. Mrs Siponen came shuffling out behind her husband, a stumpy-legged, extremely fat woman – so fat, in fact, that her Wellington boots wouldn't fit over her calves; each pair of boots had to be slit to halfway before she could get them on. The mistress of the house wished the miller good morning, looked up at the clock and asked, 'What's going on at the mill to send our Kunnari out on the roads at this time of night?'

Huttunen sat down at the parlour table, lit a cigarette and offered one to Siponen who was putting on a pair of trousers.

'Oh, nothing, thanks for asking,' Huttunen replied. 'No, I just thought I'd drop by. It's a long time since I've come round.'

The farmer sat down opposite Huttunen, smoking his cigarette with a cardboard filter. He peered into the miller's eyes in silence, leaning forward short-sightedly. Launola went out behind the house, came back in and, as nobody said anything to him, got back into his bunk, turned his face to the wall and soon began snoring.

'Is the adviser home?' Huttunen eventually asked.

'I think she's upstairs, asleep,' Siponen said, pointing to the attic.

Huttunen put out his cigarette and started up the stairs. The farmer and his wife remained sitting at the table, looking at one another in bewilderment. They heard the miller's heavy tread on the stairs, a thud as he banged his head on the ceiling at the top, then a knock, a woman's voice, and a door closing. Mrs Siponen hurried over to the foot of the stairs to listen to what was being said upstairs, but she couldn't hear a thing.

'Go up further, you'll be able to hear better,' her husband told her, 'but don't make the stairs squeak. Go on, up you go, and tell me what you can hear. But don't make them squeak! For God's sake! I can't believe I'm married to a woman who makes the whole house shake.'

In a daze of sleep and surprise, the horticulture adviser invited Huttunen into her little room in her nightgown. The miller stooped forward under the sloping ceiling, his cap in one hand, the other held out in greeting.

'Good morning, Miss Adviser . . . Sorry to come and see you at a time like this, but I thought I'd be sure to find you at home. I've heard that you're out travelling all over the canton from morning till night giving your advice.'

'I'm definitely at home at this time of day. What is it, actually? Ah, not yet five.'

'I hope I didn't wake you,' Huttunen said anxiously.

'It's all right . . . Please sit down, Mr Huttunen, don't stay standing bent over double like that. This room has such a low ceiling. The bigger ones with higher ceilings were too expensive.'

'It's a pretty room . . .' Huttunen commented. 'I don't even have curtains at the mill – I mean, not in my bedroom. You don't really need them in the mill itself.'

He sat down on a little stool next to the stove. He wanted to light a cigarette but thought better of it; it didn't seem appropriate to smoke in a woman's room. The adviser sat on the edge of the bed and pushed her tangled curls off her forehead. She looked lovely with the traces of sleep still clinging to her. Her full breasts swelled under her nightgown; the neckline revealed the shadowy beginnings of her cleavage. Huttunen had trouble tearing his eyes away.

'I've been waiting every day thinking you'd come to the mill, Miss. I planted the garden immediately, like we said. I thought you'd come and see me.'

'I was planning to next week,' Sanelma Käyrämö laughed nervously.

'It seemed such a long time,' Huttunen went on, 'and the seeds haven't come up yet.'

The adviser quickly explained that they couldn't have come up because they'd only been planted a few days before; that Mr Huttunen shouldn't be too impatient and that he could return to the mill quite secure in the knowledge that the vegetables would be up in their own good time.

'Should I be going then?' he asked piteously, not wanting to go anywhere.

'I'll come and see your garden at the beginning of next week,' the horticulture adviser promised. 'This is an unusual time for a visit and I am a lodger here. Even though she is such a large person, Mrs Siponen is very strict.'

'What if I sat here for just half an hour?' Huttunen ventured, trying to delay the moment of departure.

'Please try to understand, Mr Huttunen.'

'But I only came, Miss,' the miller protested, 'because you said that if I had any problems I could come and see you.'

Sanelma Käyrämö was at a loss as to what to do. She would gladly have let this strange, handsome man stay sitting next to the stove, but it was out of the question. She thought it was funny she wasn't afraid of this curious fellow, who so many people thought of as mentally ill. But anyway, for the moment she had to get him to leave; his visit couldn't go on and on. What would they think downstairs if he stayed any longer?

'Let's see each other during my working hours . . . at the shop or the café. Or out and about, in the woods – anywhere, except here, at this hour.'

'I suppose I should go then.'

Huttunen sighed heavily, put on his cap and shook the adviser's hand. Sanelma Käyrämö was certain the poor man was in love with her, he looked so wretched at having to leave.

'Goodbye, Mr Huttunen. We'll see each other again soon under more favourable circumstances.'

The burden of Huttunen's sorrow eased slightly. He gripped the door handle resolutely and, with a polite bow to the horticulture adviser, gave the door a firm push. It struck something soft and heavy. There was a terrible scream, followed by a tremendous crash. Mrs Siponen had heaved herself up to the top of the stairs to listen to their conversation and when the miller opened the door, it hit her smack behind the ear and sent her flying down the steep stairs. Luckily she was as round as a barrel and she rolled softly all the way to the bottom of the stairs where the farmer found her. However, blood was trickling from her ear and she was screaming so loudly the windowpanes rattled.

The farmhand Launola ran out from the parlour. Huttunen came down the stairs, followed by the horticulture adviser. The farmer's wife lay groaning on the floor. Mr Siponen gave Huttunen a savage look and yelled, 'What in hell's name do you think you're doing, barging in on honest people in the middle of the night and trying to kill the mistress of the house?'

'She's not dead yet. Let's get her to bed,' Launola said.

They lugged the farmer's wife to the back room and lifted her onto the bed. Then Huttunen left the house, jumped on his bike and shot out of the farmyard, pedalling furiously. The farmer followed him out onto the porch, shouting, 'If my wife is paralysed, Kunnari, you'll have to pay for her care! I'll take you to court!'

The Siponens' dog barked uninterruptedly until dawn.

CHAPTER 6

Huttunen contemplated his vegetable patch all the following week without daring to show his face in the village. Then suddenly his sad and lonely vigil came to an end. The horticulture adviser pedalled gaily up the mill, greeted him amiably and got straight down to discussing vegetables. The lettuces were already sprouting and the carrot shoots would soon be up, she said. She collected the money for the seeds she had given Huttunen on her previous visit and showed him how to thin the plants and loosen the soil.

'Everything is in the detail,' she insisted.

Huttunen merrily made coffee and got out biscuits.

When every angle of the vegetable patch had been covered, Sanelma Käyrämö broached the subject of the miller's visit.

'Actually, I came to talk to you about the other night,' she began.

'I won't come and see you again,' Huttunen promised, shamefaced.

Once was more than enough, the horticulture adviser pointed out. Mrs Siponen was still in bed and refusing to get up, even to look after the cows. Siponen had sent for the village doctor to examine his wife.

'Dr Ervinen listened to her chest and turned her this way and that – well, he had help for the turning bit, you know how much she weighs. He bandaged her ear and said it should be bathed; I suppose there's something wrong internally, that's where the door handle hit her. But the doctor shouted in her ear and said her hearing wasn't damaged, she was just pretending to be deaf. He shone a very powerful torch in her eyes, so close it was almost touching, and then suddenly yelled into the bad ear. He said her crystalline lens moved, which meant she could still hear. But the farmer didn't believe him. So then we all bellowed into Mrs Siponen's ear and stared into her eyes, but she remained completely expression-less. Siponen said it was going to cost Kunnari: his wife was stone deaf.'

Huttunen gave the adviser a beseeching look, hoping that that would be the end of the bad news, but Sanelma Käyrämö pressed on: 'Dr Ervinen thought Mrs Siponen should get out of bed and get back to work. But she claims she can't move any of her limbs and has to stay where she is. She's decided she's paralysed and will never be able to leave her bed again. She's adamant and there was nothing Ervinen could do. On his way out, he simply said that as far as he was concerned, she could stay in bed until the Last Judgement. Siponen is threatening to send for a better doctor who will certify his wife disabled, and keeps swearing that Kunnari will have to pay.'

So that's where matters stood, Huttunen thought sadly. Everyone knew that Mrs Siponen was the fattest, laziest woman for miles around. Now she had the perfect excuse to lounge about all day. Naturally Launola, the two-faced farmhand, would swear to any story his master and mistress wanted him to.

The horticulture adviser said she'd wanted to tell the miller because she knew he was innocent, and also because she liked him. She proposed that she and Huttunen start calling each other by their first names.

'But let's only do it when we're on our own, when no one can hear us,' she added.

This made the miller – Gunnar, as the adviser called him from then on – deliriously happy.

They helped themselves to some more coffee. Then the adviser turned to another, even more delicate, subject.

'Gunnar . . . can I ask you an extremely personal question? It's a sensitive matter that there's been a lot of talk of in the village.'

'Ask whatever you want, I won't mind.'

The horticulture adviser didn't know where to start. She took a sip of coffee, crumbled a biscuit into her cup, looked out of the mill window, and almost started talking about the vegetable garden again, before finally resolving to get straight to the point.

41

'A lot of people in the village say you're not quite normal.'

Huttunen nodded awkwardly.

'I know . . . They say I'm mad.'

'Yes. Yesterday I went to have coffee with the school-teacher's wife and she said you were insane . . . And dangerous, apparently, and who knows what else. The schoolteacher's wife said that when you were in the shop, you suddenly dragged the scales outside and put them down the well. That can't be true: people don't do things like that.'

Huttunen was forced to admit that he had put Tervola's scales down the shop's well.

'He can get them out, he only has to pull up the bucket.'

'People talk of bombs as well and howling . . . Is it true that you howl in the winter?'

Huttunen felt ashamed. He had to confess that he did howl.

'I have whined a bit now and then, but nothing nasty.'

'Apparently you imitate different animals . . . and you make fun of the villagers, of Siponen, Vittavaara, the teacher and the shopkeeper. Is that true too?'

Huttunen explained that sometimes he just felt the need to do something special.

'It's like a jolt in the brain. But I'm not a danger to anyone.'

The horticulture adviser remained silent for a long time. Deeply touched, she looked sadly at the miller sitting opposite her with his coffee.

'If only I could do something to help,' she said finally, taking Huttunen's hand in hers. 'I think that's awful, someone howling all on their own.'

The miller coughed and blushed. Thanking him for the coffee, the adviser stood up to leave.

'Don't go yet,' Huttunen blurted out. 'Don't you like it here?'

'If people find out I'm spending a lot of time here, I'll lose my job,' Sanelma explained. 'I really have to go.'

'If I stop howling, will you come back?' Huttunen asked, and then hurriedly suggested that if Sanelma didn't dare come and see him at the mill, why didn't they meet some-where else, in the woods, for instance? He promised to find a place where they could see each other from time to time without being disturbed.

The horticulture adviser hesitated.

'It has to be somewhere safe and not too far away so I won't get lost,' she said. 'I can only come to the mill twice a month. If I come more often, people will start talking, and the 4H Association could lose patience.'

Huttunen took the adviser in his arms. She didn't object. The miller murmured in her ear that he wasn't so mad that a person couldn't hit it off with him. Then he thought of a suitable meeting place. There was a little stream that ran under the church road; if Sanelma followed this for half a mile on the north bank, she'd get to a point where the stream bent sharply and split into two branches around an islet covered with a dense grove of alders. No one ever went onto Leppäsaari Island,

Huttunen said. It was a lovely, peaceful place, not too far.

'I'll fell a couple of trunks to make a bridge so you'll be able to get across without gumboots.'

The horticulture adviser agreed to come to the island the following Sunday, provided that Huttunen did not get into any more trouble.

Huttunen meekly promised to behave.

'I'll stay quietly in the mill and I won't howl, however much I want to.'

The horticulture adviser urged Huttunen to water his vegetable patch every evening – they were having such a dry, hot summer – and then she rode off. Left on his own, the radiantly happy Huttunen looked at the mill's grey wooden walls and thought that they could do with a bit of sprucing up. He decided to paint his mill red.

CHAPTER 7

Huttunen rigged up a twenty-gallon drum in front of the mill, lit a fire underneath it and set a mixture of water, red ochre, rye flour and other ingredients of house paint to boil, stirring them continuously and keeping the heat steady. He was in buoyant spirits, full of optimism and energy; the day after tomorrow would be Sunday and he would be seeing the horticulture adviser on Leppäsaari Island.

With plenty of time to spare, the miller had made a bridge over the stream out of a couple of logs. He had put up a tent and a mosquito net in the copse on the edge of a small clearing like a sort of garden, and covered the ground with hay. There wouldn't be any insects disturbing the adviser in that cool shelter. It drives women crazy, being bitten by mosquitoes; Sanelma is bound to like what I've done, Huttunen thought happily.

Mixing with the yellowy brown rye flour, the red ochre began to produce a beautiful oxblood colour. The paint would be ready that evening, and he could finish the whole mill by Sunday. It wouldn't have cost much. The flour came from his own supplies; all he'd had to buy was the red ochre and some iron sulphate.

At that moment, his neighbour Vittavaara reined in his horse in front of the mill. Huttunen saw the portly farmer was perched on one of half a dozen sacks of grain stacked in his cart. Delighted that he had brought him last year's harvest to mill, the miller put some more wood on the fire under the drum and went over to help the farmer hitch his horse to the post on the mill wall.

'You've decided to have a go at painting, then,' Vittavaara observed, as they carried the sacks into the mill. 'I saw at the churchyard gate that your mill was working, so I've brought the rest of my barley . . . We've got to support our own mill. Can't let all that good river water slip past lazily for free and go to waste somewhere else.'

Huttunen started up the mill, opened the first sack and emptied it into the hopper. The air was soon thick with the smell of freshly ground barley. The men went outside. Huttunen offered Vittavaara a cigarette, thinking to himself that here at last was a decent neighbour he could actually get on with. A different sort of person altogether to that Siponen and his bone-idle wife.

'You've got a beautiful gelding there,' Huttunen enthused, to show the goodwill he bore its owner.

'He's a bit skittish, but otherwise he's a good horse,' Vittavaara replied, and then cleared his throat. Huttunen sensed that his neighbour had something else on his mind besides getting some old barley milled. Did he have a message from Siponen? Or the shopkeeper Tervola, or the teacher?

'Listen, speaking man to man . . . as one good neighbour to another, I want to warn you, Kunnari. You're a good fellow all round, that goes without saying, but you do have one failing. It's come up at social services – I'm head of the board in fact.'

Huttunen dropped his cigarette and trod it into the ground. What was Vittavaara driving at, he wondered warily.

'How can I put it?' Vittavaara hesitated. 'There are so many people in the commune who have a grievance against you. You've absolutely got to stop your howling and all your other carrying on. There have been complaints about you all the way up to the board.'

Huttunen looked his neighbour fiercely in the eye.

'Tell me plainly what people have been saying about me.'

'I've told you. The howling has to stop, once and for all. It's not right that a grown man should be out barking with the dogs. Last winter you kept the whole village awake for nights on end, and now you've done it again. My wife couldn't sleep all spring because of you, and my children have got problems at school. My daughter had to re-sit a special end-of-year exam – that's what happens

47

when you stay awake all night and spend all the summer in the mill listening to your foolishness.'

'I howled less than usual this spring,' Huttunen volunteered in his defence. 'I only really let rip a few times.'

'You insult people, you play the clown, you make fun of everyone. Even the teacher Tanhumäki has brought it up. You imitate all sorts of animals and then, on top of everything, you have to go and throw bombs in the river.'

'It was a joke.'

Vittavaara had got the bit between his teeth now. The veins on his forehead bulged as he railed against Huttunen.

'And you have the nerve to protest, for Christ's sake! As if I hadn't spent thousands of nights on the edge of my bed listening to you moaning in your mill – like this. Listen, does this ring any bells?'

Absolutely livid, Vittavaara started to howl, throwing up his arms and staring at the sky. A high-pitched wail burst from his throat, so piercing that his horse took fright.

'That's how you terrified the whole canton. You maniac! And all your buffoonery! When you pretend to be a bear or an elk or a bloody snake or crane, have a look, just for a joke, just have a look at what it looks like. Watch closely! Is this any way for a human being to behave?'

Vittavaara rocked heavily from foot to foot like a bear, growling and slashing with his claws, before throwing himself down on all fours and roaring so irately that his gelding strained at the bit.

'That was the bear, probably rings a few bells. Then how about this one? You've done this one a few times!'

Vittavaara trotted around the drum of paint, snorting and grunting like a reindeer, halted with a shake of his head, pawed the grass and bent down as if he were grazing lichen. Then he switched from a reindeer to a lemming. He rubbed his mouth, sat up on his hind legs and squealed aggressively in Huttunen's direction, before scampering off under the cart like a rodent in a towering fury.

'Stop this minute,' Huttunen cried, finally losing patience. 'You don't know if you're coming or going. A man who doesn't even know how to do a proper imitation! Bloody hell, I may have imitated a bear but I never did it so bloody clumsily.'

Vittavaara took a deep breath and tried to calm down.

'I was just trying to say that if you don't change your ways, the board will put a muzzle on you and have you sent to Oulu mental hospital. We've already discussed it with Ervinen. The doctor told me you were mentally ill. Manic depression. You even hit Mrs Siponen one night and made her deaf. Remember? You stole the shopkeeper's scales and threw them down the well. Tervola has had to make a rough guess measuring out his flour for the past few days, and it's cost him money.'

Huttunen flew into a fury. What gave this man the right to come to his mill and berate and threaten him? He nearly punched Vittavaara in his jowly face, but at the last minute he remembered Sanelma Käyrämö's warning.

'Get your barley out of here, every last grain of it!' the miller shouted instead. 'I won't mill an ounce of flour for someone of your sort. And for Christ's sake take that nag with you or I'll shoo it into the river.'

Vittavaara was icily calm.

'You'll mill what you're told to mill. There are still laws in this world and I am going to teach you them. You may have howled down south, but that isn't going to wash here. I hope you understand that, because I won't be telling you twice.'

Huttunen ran into the mill and turned off the engine. He emptied the bin of flour that had already been milled onto the ground, scuffing up clouds of it with his feet, and swung the hopper away from the runner stone. Then he slung one of the unopened sacks onto his back, ran out to the mill bridge, drew his knife from his belt and gutted it. He shook the barley out into the rapids and chucked the remains of the sack after it. The rest went straight into the river without further ado.

Vittavaara unhitched his terrified gelding and led him out onto the road. From there, he shouted at the miller, 'You've pulled your last stunt, Kunnari! You've ruined five sacks of top quality barley! You haven't heard the last of this!'

Huttunen spat at the waterlogged sacks of grain floating in the river. The mill stood silently in its place, the drum of red ochre steaming at its feet. Huttunen grabbed the ladle of fiery red paint and charged at Vittavaara. The farmer whipped up his horse with the tip of the reins, and, with a squeal of the cart's rubber wheels, the gelding tore off at a gallop. The farmer's threats merged with the pounding of hooves.

'There are laws for lunatics too, damn you! Barking mad, that's what you are, you crook!'

The river carried off Vittavaara's grain. Huttunen went back to the mill exhausted. With a grouse feather brush, he swept up the flour on the floor and threw it out of the window into the rapids.

CHAPTER 8

Constable Portimo, a venerable figure in both the village and the constabulary, pedalled out sedately to the Suukoski mill on his old bicycle with its specially fitted low-pressure tyres. Freewheeling down the last of the hills, he saw that Huttunen had started painting his property. One wall was already done. The miller was perched on a ladder on the other side, above the bridge, slapping red paint onto the grey logs.

'This won't be a wasted journey. Kunnari's home,' Constable Portimo thought idly and leant his bicycle against the mill's still unpainted southern wall.

'You've got started on some home improvements, then,' he called out to Huttunen who came down the ladder with his pot of paint.

The men took out their cigarettes. Huttunen gave Portimo a light, thinking that Vittavaara, damn him, must have gone and reported the grain he'd thrown in the river. After a few drags, he asked, 'Are you out on official business?'

'A police constable with no land hasn't got any grain to bring to the mill. It's about the business with Vittavaara.'

After finishing his cigarette and exhausting the subject of the mill's new coat of paint, Constable Portimo moved on to his official mission. He took a bill out of his wallet and handed it to Huttunen, who read that he owed Vittavaara the equivalent of five sacks of grain. The miller went inside to get a pen and some money, paid the bill and signed it at the bottom. The price wasn't very high but still he told Portimo, 'Most of it was sprouted. It would have ended up in the river, anyway. Even pigs wouldn't have eaten that.'

The constable counted the money, tucked it and the receipt into his wallet, then spat thoughtfully into the mill-race.

'Don't get on your high horse, Kunnari. When the chief came round about Vittavaara's grain, he said you ought to be locked up. I managed to calm him down and reach a compromise. Come on, be honest, Kunnari, Vittavaara basically had some good reasons for coming to see you. He wanted to talk to you about your mad fits, didn't he?'

'He's the one who's mad.'

'He told the chief he'd been to the doctor. Ervinen's promised to sign your committal papers. If he does that, then it's just a question of catching you and packing you off to the nuthouse in Oulu. If I were you, I'd try to control myself a little. There's the business with the Siponens. And then apparently at the shop you put the scales down the well. The schoolteacher's wife came to tell me about that, and Tervola telephoned too, of course. He said he had to take the scales to bits and that they aren't as accurate now as before. According to him, customers don't completely trust him anymore. There's arguments about the price of a pound every day at the shop.'

'Have you got another bill for the scales? Hand it over. I'll pay for the bloody scales too.'

Constable Portimo walked across the bridge to the water-wheel and jumped down onto the bank near the shingle saw; a little water got into one of his boots. He walked along the edge of millrace to the dam, with Huttunen following. On the dam, the policeman shook the sturdy wooden piles to see if they'd budge, but they were firmly anchored in the riverbed.

'You've really done this mill up a treat,' Portimo said admiringly. 'It's never been in this good shape, apart from when it was new, of course. I can still remember it being built on these rapids. It was in '02. I was six then. There's been a lot of grain milled here. It only became really derelict in the war. It's good you've repaired it and we don't have to go to Kemi or Liedakkala for shingles or flour anymore.'

Huttunen enthusiastically related that he was planning to replace the last section of the millrace. And that wasn't all.

'I thought I could hook up a band saw as well. The current is easily strong enough. It just needs a new wheel here, or you make the shingle saw's wheel bigger and run a driving belt behind it. You'd have to raise up the saw so the head rig was close enough. If the belt's too long and comes off, it can kill you. A lot of sawyers get cut to pieces that way.'

The policeman considered the potential site of the saw with a doubtful air. Huttunen elaborated: 'Sixty cartloads of stone and sand there and you've got the base for a saw. There, higher up, you can put a stacking system and there's plenty of room to store the logs, no matter how much sawing you do.'

'Yes, now I see. But you can't cut logs and shingle at the same time.'

'Of course not, if you use the same wheel. But I am on my own here.'

'True enough.'

Constable Portimo pictured the new saw. He looked Huttunen benevolently in the eye, and said gravely, 'With all your plans, and now the mill's in such good condition, you should try not to be so foolish. That's the advice of a friend. If they make me take you to Oulu, the mill will fall to pieces again and who knows what sort of character we'll get instead of you.'

Huttunen earnestly nodded in agreement. The men walked back from the dam. Portimo took his bicycle from the mill wall and waved to Huttunen as he rode off. The miller thought that Portimo was definitely the most amiable soul in the village, even if he was a policeman.

Portimo reminded him of Sanelma Käyrämö. They were equally kind and understanding. Huttunen would be seeing the adviser on Leppäsaari Island tomorrow, provided it didn't rain. On the radio they had promised it would stay dry until the evening; luckily there was an anti-cyclone over Fennoscandia.

Huttunen went back to painting the mill. If he worked all night, in the morning a red mill would bestride the Suukoski rapids. He'd heard some women from Helsinki were touring the country with a revue called that, *The Red Mill.* They'd come up to Kemi and Rovaniemi; apparently their skirts were so short you could see their knickers and suspenders.

It was agreeable painting in the cool, clear summer night. Huttunen was tired but he didn't feel sleepy. He had two fine subjects to occupy his mind: the mill's beautiful new livery and tomorrow's meeting with the horticulture adviser on the island in the middle of the stream. He worked flat out all night. When the Sunday morning sun lit up the northeastern wall of the mill, the job was done. The miller took the ladder and the few remaining pots of red paint to the shed. He bathed in the river and then walked round his building twice, admiring its beauty. What a dapper mill!

Delighted, Huttunen went into the mill house to have some Finnish sausage and a glass of buttermilk. Then he set off for Leppäsaari Island. It was still early in the morning and the tired miller fell asleep on the hay in the cool of the tent, a happy, trusting smile on his face.

CHAPTER 9

Huttunen was woken by a rustling of the mosquito net. He heard a timid woman's voice outside.

'Gunnar . . . I'm here.'

The miller stuck out a sleepy head, and pulled the hesitant adviser into the white, sweet-smelling tent. She was in a fever of nerves, hurriedly telling him all sorts of things: she shouldn't really have come; they oughtn't to see each other like this; Siponen's wife was still in bed and firmly resolved never to get up again; what time was it anyway; and oh . . . my goodness, wasn't it a beautiful day, though?

Huttunen and the adviser sat on the hay, looked into one another's eyes and held hands. Huttunen would have liked to take her in his arms but she pulled back when he tried.

'I haven't come here for that,' she said.

Huttunen made do with stroking her knee. Sanelma Käyrämö reflected that she was now alone on a deserted island in the depths of the forest with a mentally ill person. How had she dared take such a risk? Gunnar Huttunen could do whatever he wanted with her without anyone being able to stop him. He could strangle her, rape her. Where would he hide the body? He'd tie stones to her feet and throw her into the stream, obviously. Only her hair would float free in the swirling current – luckily she didn't have a perm. But what if Gunnar chopped her up in pieces and buried her? Sanelma Käyrämo imagined the knife marks on her neck and her wrists and her thighs . . . She shivered, but not enough to take her hand out of the miller's.

Huttunen meanwhile looked adoringly into her eyes.

'I painted the mill this week. Red. Constable Portimo came to have a look yesterday.'

The horticulture adviser gave a start. What did the police officer want? Huttunen told her about Vittavaara's grain, adding that he'd paid for it.

'The police chief made me pay bread flour prices for sprouted grain. Luckily there were only five sacks.'

The horticulture adviser began fervently trying to convince Huttunen that he absolutely had to go and see Dr Ervinen. Didn't Gunnar understand that he was ill?

'Dear Gunnar, your mental equilibrium is at stake. I beg you, please go and talk to Ervinen.'

'Ervinen's just a village doctor. What does he know about mental illness, he's mad himself,' Huttunen protested half-heartedly.

'But what if you went there to ask him for some medicine say, because you can't control yourself. They've got tranquillisers now; Ervinen can prescribe you some. If you haven't got the money, I can lend it to you.'

'I'm embarrassed to tell the doctor about my problems,' Huttunen said wearily, taking his hand out of the adviser's. She looked at him tenderly, stroking his hair and letting her fingers linger on his high, hot forehead. She thought that if she slept with the miller now, she'd definitely have a child. She'd fall pregnant instantly. It wasn't a safe time of the month. But was there ever a safe time for a woman, a really safe one? A man that tall just had to touch you and you'd have a child. A boy. She didn't really dare think of it. First her stomach would start swelling, and then by autumn it would be hard to ride her bicycle. The 4H Association wouldn't give her any leave under the circumstances. Thank goodness her father had died in the Winter War; he wouldn't have been able to stand it.

The horticulture adviser thought of the sort of child she'd have with the miller: a fat baby with thick hair and a long nose. He'd be at least three foot at birth. No one would dare breastfeed him, this deranged cherub fathered by a lunatic. He wouldn't burble away like an ordinary newborn, but would howl like his father. Or whine at least. Normal children's clothes wouldn't fit him; she'd have to sew him sailor trousers to wear in his cot. He'd grow a beard by the time he was five and howl during morning prayers at school. In biology lessons he'd

61

imitate all sorts of animals and the teacher Tanhumäki would have to send him out in the middle of the lesson. She wouldn't dare go and have coffee with the school-teacher's wife anymore. The rest of the day Huttunen's son would hang around the village, tearing election posters off the telegraph poles. And then what would he get up to with his father in the evenings? What a nightmare!

'No. I really do have to go. I shouldn't have come at all. Who knows if somebody hasn't see me, anyway.'

Huttunen put his hand on the horticulture adviser's shoulder. She stayed in the tent.

* * *

What was it that was so calm and reassuring about this man that you couldn't tear yourself away from him? Sanelma Käyrämö had no desire to leave. She would gladly have stayed all day in that cool, white shelter, even all night. She thought to herself that as a rule she was terrified of mad people, but not this one. Gunnar had powers of seduction for which there was no rational explanation.

'It would be awful if they came and took you off to Oulu.'

'I am not as mad as all that.'

The horticulture adviser said nothing. In her opinion, Gunnar Huttunen was easily mad enough to be committed to Oulu. She had heard enough conversations about 'that lunatic Kunnari'. If only they could be completely alone, and no one ever see them! Gunnar Huttunen's fits of madness struck a chord with the horticulture adviser; she almost found them funny; she certainly didn't blame him for them. What can you do about the way your brain works? The villagers just didn't understand him, that was all.

Sanelma Käyrämö began imagining them getting married. Gunnar would lead her to the altar: they'd have the ceremony in the canton's old church: the new one was too big and gloomy. Saint Michael's Day would be a good date for the wedding. She didn't have enough time to make a dress for Midsummer. Gunnar would have to get a dark suit made as well; it could do for funerals afterwards. So. A Midsummer wedding, and then the baby born next spring, which would be perfect timing. Spring babies are adorable, and vegetable juice in summer is an ideal supplement to their milk. By this point, the horticulture adviser was thinking of her baby as a sweet little pink-cheeked girl.

All three of them would live in the tiny mill house. The baby would fall asleep at night, lulled by the murmuring of the stream. She would never cry, and Gunnar would sometimes put her to bed himself. Her little cot, made by the miller, would be a shiny, bright blue. Sanelma could bring the curtains and the grained birch dresser from the Siponens' attic room to start off with. They'd have to put up a flower-shaped wall light in the parlour and arrange wicker armchairs for four beneath it. Or for two, at least. They'd put the radio on the windowsill so that people could see it from outside. The bedroom had to have a double bed with bedside tables either side. One with a mirror. As the young lady of the house, she would sweep the floors and beat the carpets every week. They would buy a rattle from Tervola's. Sometimes the whole family would go shopping; Gunnar would push the pram on the way there, and if he stayed to have a pilsner and talk business afterwards, that would be fine. She could walk back some of the way with the schoolteacher's wife.

No, it was all impossible. If she didn't leave this tent soon, she'd have a baby, the mad child of a mad man. And yet still the horticulture adviser couldn't bring herself to go. She lay in the sweet-smelling tent with the miller all Sunday until evening. They were happy, talking about this and that, holding hands; Huttunen stroked her calves. It was only when the evening grew cooler that the miller walked the adviser back to the main road, from where she rode off on her bicycle to the Siponens. Deep in thought, he walked off in the opposite direction towards the Suukoski rapids.

That was a good day. Oh, how I love the adviser!

The setting sun bathed the mill in such a beautiful blaze of light that the miller wanted to howl with all his might, giving voice to all the joy and love in his heart. But then he remembered Sanelma had insisted he go and see Dr Ervinen. He pumped up the back tyre of his bike and hopped on. It was almost eleven, but the miller was not sleepy.

CHAPTER 10

Ervinen lived in an old wooden house opposite the church-yard at the end of a long avenue of birch trees. He had his medical practice and bachelor flat under the one roof. When Huttunen knocked on his front door, the doctor opened in person. He was a thin, vigorous man in his fifties. As befitted the late hour, he was wearing a smoking jacket and slippers.

'Hello, Doctor. I've come for a consultation,' said Huttunen.

Ervinen showed his patient in. The miller looked around the room, the walls of which were hung with numerous hunting scenes. Above the mantelpiece, there were stuffed animal heads, and animal skins covered the walls and floor. The predominant smell was of pipe smoke. Soberly masculine, the room served as lounge, library and dining room simultaneously. The housework clearly hadn't been done for a long time, but Huttunen found it an inviting set-up.

Stroking an elk skin spread out in front of the armchair in which he had sat down, the miller asked the doctor if he'd shot all the animals whose hides were displayed in such profusion.

'I killed the better part of them myself, but there are some trophies that have come down to me from my late father. This lynx here, for example, and that pine marten on the mantelpiece. Hard to find them these days, they're fairly rare now. I've mainly shot birds up here in the north. And of course I've shot foxes and a few elk with the council secretary.'

His voice catching with passion, Ervinen described how once during the war he had bagged almost thirty elk with his major in East Karelia. Ervinen was a battalion doctor at the time, so could move around pretty much at will. He had done plenty of fishing too, with prolific results.

'On the Äänättijoki, Major Kaarakka and I once caught sixteen salmon!'

Huttunen said that, speaking for himself, he'd caught a fair few trout and grayling in the millstream last autumn. Did the doctor know how well stocked the streams were, especially the upper reaches?

Ervinen began pacing up and down the room with excitement. He rarely had the chance to talk about hunting and fishing with someone who knew anything about it, and all the signs were that the miller was a master of these arts. Ervinen exclaimed that it was a damn shame that the Isohaara dam had been built across the mouth of the Kemijoki so you didn't get salmon swimming upstream to spawn anymore. It would be extremely agreeable landing a salmon in one's net and grilling it over a fire on the riverbank. But the nation needed electricity. And when a choice had to be made between a lesser evil and a greater good, it was the latter that necessarily prevailed.

Ervinen took two stemmed glasses out of the corner sideboard and filled them with a transparent liquid. Bringing his glass to his lips, Huttunen realised the concoction was rectified spirit. It burned every inch of the way down his long throat, boring a path to the pit of his stomach where it gently lapped back and forth, a pool of fire. He was instantly suffused with a feeling of profound wellbeing and respectful camaraderie for the doctor, who was now talking about hare coursing and the ideal dogs for that sport. After this he showed Huttunen his collection of hunting rifles that covered an entire wall: a Japanese army rifle converted into a heavy hunting rifle; a Sako rifle; what's known as a parlour rifle; and two shotguns.

'I've only got a single-barrelled Russian shotgun myself,' Huttunen said modestly. 'But I'm thinking of getting a rifle this autumn. I've already been to the chief to ask for a permit, in fact, last winter, but he turned me down. He said he should've already come and collected my shotgun as it was, whatever that meant. But I'm more of a fisherman really.'

Ervinen hung his weapons back on the wall. Then he

drained his glass and, in a more official tone of voice, inquired, 'So what seems to be our miller's problem?'

'The thing is, people say I'm a bit d-disturbed . . . Who knows really.'

Ervinen sat in a rocking chair covered with a bearskin and studied Huttunen awhile. Then he nodded benevolently and said, 'There is something in what they say. I'm only a GP but I don't think I'd be too far off the mark if I diagnosed you as depressive.'

Huttunen felt ill at ease. He found it acutely embarrassing talking about these things. He knew that he wasn't completely normal, and he was happy to admit it; he'd always known. But he was damned if it had anything to do with anyone else. Depressive . . . maybe that's what he was. Depressive. Then what?

'Are there pills for this sort of illness? Can the doctor prescribe me some so everyone in the village will calm down?'

This was a very affecting case he had here, Ervinen thought. A man of the people afflicted by a congenital nervous illness, benign, certainly, but pronounced. What could he do for him? Nothing. A man like that should marry and forget the whole thing. But where was a madman going to find a wife? Women were scared enough of a man that tall as it was.

'I'd like to ask as a doctor . . . Is it true that you're in the habit of howling at night, especially in winter?'

'I did have to whine a bit last winter, yes,' Huttunen admitted, ashamed.

'And what is it that makes our miller groan like that? Is it an obsession, such that you can't do anything else except howl?'

Huttunen wished he were somewhere else, but when Ervinen repeated the question, he had to give an answer.

'It . . . it comes out automatically. First I have a sort of need to shout. My head feels tight, and then it has to come out, very loud. It's not completely out of control, it's just something that comes over me when I'm on my own. It's always a relief afterwards. A few howls are enough.'

Ervinen turned the conversation to Huttunen's propensity to imitate animals and people. Where did this come from? What did this behaviour mean to the miller?

'I just feel so perky sometimes that I want to lark around, but it often gets out of hand, I'm sure. Most of the time I'm quite gloomy. I don't do those imitations very often.'

'And when you're in a black mood, you have the urge to howl,' Ervinen put in incisively.

'Yes, at those times, it helps.'

'Do you ever talk to yourself?'

'When I'm in a good mood, sometimes I chat away about this and that,' Huttunen admitted.

Ervinen went to the corner cupboard and took out a little bottle, which he handed to the miller. He said it contained pills, which Huttunen could take when he felt very depressed, but he had to be careful not to take too many. One a day was enough.

'They're from the war. It's not actually legal to make them anymore. They'll definitely do the trick, but you must only take them if you feel really bad. Only if you really feel you're on the brink of howling.'

Huttunen put the bottle in his pocket and stood up to leave. But Ervinen said he had no plans to go to bed yet; his guest could have another drink if he liked. He poured the miller a hefty shot of rectified spirit, and then refilled his own glass.

The men drank in silence. Then Ervinen resumed talking about hunting. He described going to Turtola with two keeshonds late one winter before the wars. They had gone to hunt bear, which still spent the winter in Turtola in those days. Ervinen had hired a local man as a guide. The fellow had taken him with his horse along a forest track to a circle drawn in the snow around the bear's lair. They'd left the horse half a mile away and skied back with the dogs on the leash.

'It's incredible how exciting one's first bear hunt can be. It's more exhilarating than going into battle.'

'I can imagine,' said Huttunen, drinking a mouthful of spirits.

Ervinen topped up their glasses before continuing.

'I had really fantastic dogs. The minute they caught the scent of the bear's lair, they flew at it! Snow went flying as they charged in, like this!'

Ervinen went down on all fours on the carpet to imitate the hunting dogs attacking the bear asleep in its den.

'At that point, the damn bear came dashing out. It

didn't have a choice. The dogs immediately leapt on its haunches, like this!'

Growling furiously, Ervinen sunk his teeth into the hindquarters of the bearskin draped over the rocking chair, sending it flying. He dragged the hide across the floor, his mouth full of fur.

'Couldn't shoot, might hit the dogs.'

With mounting excitement, the doctor spat out some bear fur, refilled their glasses in a blink of an eye and went on with his story. He imitated the dogs and the bear at bay by turns, throwing himself into his performance with such ardour that he was soon bathed in sweat. When he finally managed to kill the bear, he reached down into its throat and symbolically cut out its tongue at the base and flung it to the dogs – so brutally that the ashtray spilled over on the table, but the hunter didn't care. He plunged his knife into the bear's chest, staining the snow with the king of the forests' blood, and bent down over the imaginary carcass to drink the beast's warm blood, but as there wasn't any in reality, he tossed a glass of rectified spirit down the hatch instead. Finally he got to his feet and, purple in the face, went and sat in the rocking chair.

The scene had made such a strong impression on Huttunen that he couldn't control himself any longer and leapt out of his chair to imitate a crane.

'The other summer at Posio I saw a crane in the marshes. It was strutting about and trumpeting, like this, and skewering frogs in a waterhole, which it would gulp down like this, whoops!'

Huttunen demonstrated how the crane pinned the marsh frogs with its bill, how it stretched out its big neck and lifted its feet, as it screeched its shrill cries.

The doctor watched the performance in stunned silence. He couldn't understand what had got into his patient. Was the miller making fun of him or was the man really mad enough to suddenly start imitating a crane he hadn't even shot? Huttunen's piercing trumpeting infuriated Ervinen. Deciding that the unstable miller must have taken it into his deranged mind to make fun of his host, the doctor got up from his seat and said in a strained voice, 'Stop, my good man. I will not tolerate such clowning in my house.'

Huttunen stopped screeching. He calmed down immediately, saying he hadn't meant to annoy the doctor in the slightest. He was just showing how the forest's animals behaved in their natural habitat.

'The doctor imitated a bear. It was a fine sight!'

Ervinen lost his temper. He had simply illustrated a hunting incident; that didn't mean that one immediately had to follow suit in such a ridiculous and tasteless fashion. No one had the right to play the fool under his roof.

'Get out!'

Huttunen was dumbfounded. Was that all it took to upset the doctor? Strange how highly strung people turned out to be when it came down to it. The miller tried to apologise, but Ervinen wouldn't hear another word on the subject. He stiffly showed him the door, refused to take any money for the pills and moved the half-finished glass out of his reach.

Huttunen hurried out, his ears ringing. Shocked and embarrassed, he ran across the garden to the avenue of birch trees, forgetting his bicycle. Coming out onto the doorstep to watch his patient leave, the doctor saw his tall silhouette dash off towards the graveyard. 'Now lunatics think they can make fun of you. And that man doesn't know a thing about hunting either. What a peasant!'

CHAPTER 11

Huttunen stopped at the corner of the churchyard. His heart and stomach ached: Ervinen's rotgut in his stomach and Ervinen's contempt eating away at his heart. How could the doctor have got so annoyed? First he fills you with drink, then he flies off the handle; an unpredictable sort, Huttunen thought.

The miller wanted to let out all his pain, but how could he dare howl?

He suddenly remembered the tablets Ervinen had given him. He took the bottle out of his pocket, unscrewed the top and poured a heap of little yellow pills into the crook of his palm. How many were you meant to take again? Could such ridiculously small tablets have any effect at all?

Huttunen tossed half a handful of tablets into his mouth. They tasted awful, but he chewed away regardless and swallowed them dry.

'Yeuuch! What a nightmare.'

Ervinen's pills were so bitter that Huttunen had to rush to the churchyard pump to drink some water. He leant against the gravestone of a certain Raasakka who'd been dead for centuries while he waited for them to start working.

The miller's brain began humming almost instantaneously. The powerful neuroleptics flooded into his alcohol-saturated bloodstream. His feeling of malaise dissipated. His heart began to beat fast and hard. Thick swarms of ideas buzzed through his mind. His forehead felt hot, his tongue dry, and he wanted to get stuck into something, anything . . . All around him, the gravestones suddenly looked like roughly hewn blocks of stone, unfinished and, what was more, just dotted about at random, with no method. It would be good to get them lined up neatly. The old trees in the graveyard had been left to grow all over the place as well. The best thing would be to cut them all down and plant new ones, properly laid out this time. Now the old wooden church with red walls struck Huttunen as funny and the big new church with its yellow boards, frankly ridiculous.

The miller burst into uproarious laughter about everything in sight: the graves; the trees; the churches; even the churchyard fence.

A brutal compulsion to act suddenly drove him out of the church gate. He remembered he'd left his bicycle at Ervinen's and ran off to the doctor's house at such speed that tears came to his eyes and his cap flew off; he left deep ruts in the sandy path as he skidded round the corner to pick up his bicycle. There she was!

Ervinen was sipping spirits by the fire and mulling over Huttunen's case. He rather regretted having lost his patience with a simple man of the people. Perhaps the miller hadn't intended anything disrespectful by his clowning? Perhaps the poor man had such an unrefined sense of humour that he couldn't help but express it in such inappropriate ways? A doctor should never lose his temper with a patient. Oh but, God, vets had it so easy! In a case like this, a vet could simply diagnose the animal as mad, or that its nerves had gone, and have it put down. And that would be that: the farmer would kill his cow or horse, and the representative of the animal kingdom would never cause its physician a problem again.

Depressed, Ervinen closed his eyes only to open them again immediately, as a muffled thud on the other side of the wall made him jump. The doctor recognised the miller's voice straightaway. He grabbed a rifle from the wall, knotted the belt of his smoking jacket and rushed outside, almost losing his slippers on his way.

Huttunen came marching round the house, holding his bicycle with one hand. He was in a completely different world; his eyes were sunk deep in their sockets, froth pooled at the corner of his mouth. His movements were jerky and extravagant.

'You took the pills, you maniac,' Ervinen shouted at Huttunen, who barely saw or heard him. 'Go to bed immediately, for God's sake.'

The miller brushed the doctor and his rifle aside, and leapt on the bicycle. Ditching his gun, Ervinen grabbed the bicycle rack with both hands, but Huttunen was already flying and there was no way a skinny doctor could compete. Ervinen was dragged along for twenty yards before he had to let go: his slippers were coming off and few people are crazy enough to try and stop a frenzied cyclist barefoot on gravel. Ervinen heard Huttunen storm off along the birch avenue; he couldn't make out a word of sense in his shouting.

Bawling and yelling at the top of his voice, Huttunen rode through the village. He invited himself into most of the houses and woke the occupants, shouting greetings, conversing, howling, slamming doors and kicking walls. The whole village was pandemonium. Dogs barked dementedly, women bewailed the chaos and the pastor implored the Lord.

Rural Police Chief Jaatila's telephone rang. Someone had to come and calm down the miller in the name of the law. As Jaatila was taking the call, Huttunen got to his house, ran up the steps and kicked his front door. Jaatila went to meet his visitor.

Huttunen asked for some water; his mouth was dry. But rather than give him something to drink, the police chief fetched his standard issue truncheon and boxed the miller so roundly about the ears that the poor man staggered out into the garden with stars in his eyes and went on his way clasping his head in his hands.

The police chief called Constable Portimo, who had

already heard what was going on. 'The telephone's been ringing non-stop for almost half an hour. They're saying Huttunen's having a fit.'

'Handcuff him and put him in the cell,' Jaatila said. 'Law and order have been flouted long enough in this canton.'

Constable Portimo put on his Wellington boots, loaded his pistol and gathered up a pair of handcuffs and a coil of rope. Then he set off apprehensively to find Huttunen; the miller would be in a filthy mood by now. The duties of his position sometimes struck the unassuming old policeman as extremely onerous and disagreeable.

'Please God, I beg you, make him calm down. It'd be better for everybody,' Portimo prayed.

The police constable quickly established the movements of the man he had to arrest. The summer night pulsated to Huttunen's rhythm. The most almighty racket could be heard over at the Siponens' farm, leading Portimo to deduce that the miller had paid it a visit. He had apparently not received the warmest of welcomes.

Huttunen had run into a determined group of villagers in the Siponens' farmyard: the shopkeeper Tervola, the teacher Tanhumäki, the pastor and his wife, a few parishioners of lesser standing, Mr Siponen himself and his farmhand Launola. The farm dog, which had been trained to hunt bears, was darting about under everyone's feet, trying to sink its teeth into Huttunen's behind. Horrified, the horticulture adviser Sanelma Käyrämö was watching the encounter in the shadowy yard, praying and moaning. Siponen's stricken wife had been abandoned on her bed of pain, but, refusing to countenance being left out of proceedings, she had promptly leapt up in a frenzy of curiosity and rage. Forgetting her chronic disability, she had rushed over to the window to see the throng give the mad miller of Suukoski a spectacular beating.

Pummelling him with blows and kicks, the villagers reduced Huttunen to silence. When Constable Portimo appeared, they grabbed his truncheon and dealt the miller such a thrashing that the police constable himself felt ill. With the last of his strength Huttunen managed to grab Launola's ankle, which he twisted so hard that the farmhand's shrieks of pain drowned out all the other commotion.

Eventually, outnumbered and exhausted from struggling, the miller was forced to submit. Portimo snapped the handcuffs shut on his wrists and the schoolteacher and the shopkeeper dragged their unfortunate quarry to a cart and tied him up. The pastor sat on Huttunen's head while the horse was harnessed. The miller bit the man of the cloth in the bottom, but without any unfortunate consequences, at least not for the pastor's wife. Siponen then stood on the cart and whipped up the horse, and they set off to take Huttunen to the police station.

Near the churchyard, the convoy halted as Ervinen ran out to meet them. Rifle in hand, he cried, 'Stop! I'll examine the case!'

Ervinen walked round the cart and looked the trussed-up miller in the eye. He offered an instant diagnosis: 'Stark raving mad.'

Now catatonically silent, Huttunen gazed dully at the doctor without recognising him. Ervinen searched Huttunen for the bottle of pills, nimbly transferred them to his own pocket and wiped the foam from his patient's mouth. Then he waved the posse on, saying, 'Keep him locked up. I will draw up papers for Oulu for him tomorrow.'

Siponen lashed the horse's crupper, and the cart disappeared off towards the village station. Ervinen saw Constable Portimo mop the detainee's forehead with his own handkerchief.

Returning home, the doctor shook the sand off his slippers and hung his rifle back on the wall. He put the medicine bottle he had confiscated from Huttunen back in the cupboard. Seeing how few pills were left, he shook his head sadly. He drank a medicinal shot of rectified spirit straight from the bottle and went and lay down, still wearing his old slippers.

Mrs Siponen was making coffee for the shopkeeper, the schoolteacher and the pastor, who was stroking the family's cantankerous spitz, when she suddenly remembered her incurable ailment. Solemnly smiting her breast, she collapsed on the floor, and then dragged herself off to her room, trying to look as paralysed as possible. There she bewailed the sickness that had struck her down forever, the curse that would prevent her ever leaving her bed other than feet first.

Sanelma Käyrämö couldn't sleep all that night. Burrowing under the blankets, she wept between the sheets for her darling Gunnar who had been taken from her so inexplicably. In her lonely room, the forlorn young woman's grief slowly transformed into inconsolable love.

Clapped in irons, Huttunen fell asleep in his cell. He only woke up the following day, stunned to find himself trussed up on the back seat of a car with Constable Portimo sitting next to him. Quietly, almost apologetically, the policeman told the miller, 'We're already at Simo, Kunnari.'

CHAPTER 12

The mental hospital was a vast, gloomy red-brick pile. It looked more like a barracks or a prison than a medical establishment. Constable Portimo contemplated the building and said, 'I don't like this place one bit but don't hold it against me, Kunnari. This has got nothing to do with me. I only brought you here under orders. I'd let you go if I could.'

Huttunen was registered as a patient, and given hospital clothes: a worn-out pair of pyjamas, a pair of slippers and a woolly hat. The trousers were too short, as were the sleeves. There was no belt. His money and belongings were confiscated.

The miller was led along noisy corridors to a large room already occupied by six men. He was shown a bed and told that he didn't have to fight his illness anymore; he could just quietly give in to it now. Then the door slammed and the heavy key turned in its lock. All contact with the outside world was severed. This was it, Huttunen realised. He'd finally been sent to the loony bin.

The room was cold and bleak. It was furnished with seven iron beds and a table bolted to the concrete wall. There was a tall window covered with bars that showed the hospital walls were at least three feet thick. The room's walls were veined with cracks sealed with lime. A transparent electric bulb without a shade hung from the middle of the ceiling.

The other patients were lying or sitting on their beds. They barely looked around at the arrival of a new inmate. Huttunen's neighbour on one side was a trembly old man who sat perched on the edge of his mattress, muttering incomprehensibly with his eyes closed. A slightly younger bald man, who stared unblinkingly at the corner of the room, occupied the next bed along. His neighbour was a scrawny, tearful lad, younger than the rest, with a constantly changing expression: one moment joyful, the next sad and agonised. He would knit his brows and then, seconds later, his trembling mouth would freeze in a silly, mechanical smile.

Near the door, lying on a bed away from the others, a strapping and, at first sight at least, sane and healthy-looking man was reading a book.

Two morose old men were huddled together at the end of the room, apparently wanting nothing more than each other's mournful company; they stared fixedly at one another without saying a word, just their eyes flashing.

Altogether the room emanated an air of profound despair and apathy. Huttunen tried to strike up some sort of rapport with these troubled souls. He smiled, said hello to his neighbour and asked, 'How's it going?'

No response was forthcoming. The man reading by the door was the only one even to acknowledge Huttunen. The miller asked about the habits of the place, tried to find out where everyone was from, but it was all to no avail. Wrapped up in their thoughts, his companions evinced no desire to communicate. Huttunen gave a resigned sigh and fell back onto his bed.

In the evening, a ruddy-faced orderly came into the room. His sleeves were rolled up, as if he were hoping for a fight. Full of burly energy, he asked Huttunen, 'Are you the one who was brought in this morning?'

Huttunen nodded and said he was surprised that the other patients had barely said a word to him.

'These are a pretty depressed, silent lot. New inmates are often put in here. It's better, because the agitated wing's always chaos.'

The orderly explained what the hospital expected of Huttunen.

'You behave yourself and don't start causing mayhem. We feed you twice a day. Sauna once a week. You can piss when you feel like it, there's a pot in the cupboard. If you want a shit, you tell us. The doctor comes on Mondays.'

The orderly left, locking the door behind him. Huttunen thought that it was Thursday. He wouldn't see the doctor till Monday. He had plenty of time on his hands now. He lay down on the bed and tried to go to sleep. Ervinen's pills were still working and he drowsed a little, but later, after it grew dark, sleep eluded him.

At some point, the orderly came in to tell the patients to go to bed. Everyone docilely complied. Soon the glaring electric light in the ceiling went out, having been switched off in the corridor.

The miller listened to his sleeping roommates. Two or three of them snored. The air smelled stale; someone in the corner farted from time to time. Huttunen wanted to wake him up, but then he remembered that that was where the two most unnerving patients slept.

Let them fart, the poor wretches.

Huttunen thought that anyone could go mad in a place like this if they didn't get out quickly. It was horrific to be lying in a pitch-dark room surrounded by mentally ill people. What possible use could it be? How could this incarceration cure anyone? Everything was so ordered and regulated that you couldn't make a single decision. You couldn't even go to the toilet on your own. An orderly watched to make sure no one made a mess. It was completely humiliating.

Huttunen stayed awake the first few nights. He lay sweating in his bed, tossing from side to side, and sighing. He wanted to howl but managed to control himself.

Time passed quicker during the day. Huttunen even got a few responses from some of the other patients. The skinny young guy whose expression changed constantly came and told him about his life a few times. The poor lad explained himself in such a confused way that the miller didn't understand a word. He simply nodded and agreed with everything the boy said. 'Ah yes. That's the way it is.'

There was a perpetual uproar and din in the dining room, but the meals offered some diversion to the days' monotony. Many of the patients ate with their fingers, letting the slop run down their chins; they knocked their dishes on the floor and giggled stupidly, despite being fiercely reprimanded.

A cantankerous woman who never failed to give the patients a substantial piece of her mind swept the room every day. You lazy good-for-nothings, she called them, you slovens.

'How can you be so tall and play the fool?' she scolded Huttunen.

From time to time, the orderly came in to give the inmates their medicine. He handed out the pills and made everyone take them in front of him. If someone didn't swallow their tablets straightaway, he'd roll up his sleeves, force open the recalcitrant's jaw and stuff the pills down his throat. Everyone had to take their prescribed dose, whether they liked it or not. When Huttunen asked why he wasn't given any medicine, the orderly snapped, 'The doctor will give you your prescription on Monday. Simmer down, my lad, unless you want to be taken to the agitated wing.'

Huttunen asked what it was like.

'It's agitated: like this.'

The orderly jabbed his hairy fist in the miller's face.

Huttunen jerked his head out of the way. He hated this mean-spirited, violent man who at night would shake and punch any patient who didn't jump into bed the minute he told them to. Huttunen thought that after he'd talked to the doctor on Monday and could get out of this place, he would make a mop out of this brute of an orderly and clean the corridors with him as a farewell gift. But until then he had better control himself.

On Monday Huttunen was taken to the doctor.

This was a bearded, grubby-looking figure with a tic of continually taking off his glasses and putting them back on. Now and then he would produce a dirty handkerchief from his pocket and painstakingly wipe the lenses, breathing on them and polishing them for an age. Huttunen's first impression was of a nervous, inattentive, patent imbecile.

Huttunen immediately began talking about his being discharged. Leafing through the papers on the desk in front of him, the doctor said sternly, 'But you have only just been brought in. One doesn't leave here just like that.'

'But the thing is, I'm not really mad,' Huttunen explained in his most normal voice.

'Of course you're not. Who could possibly be mad in this asylum? I'm the only one who's got any mental problems here. Everybody knows that.'

Huttunen told him he was a miller. He was urgently needed at the Suukoski rapids. He had to finish repairing the mill that summer so that it could be ready for autumn.

The doctor asked why the autumn specifically.

'Well, autumn's when the harvest's brought in in Finland, you see. That's when the farmers bring their grain to me to be milled.'

The miller's reply amused the doctor. He took off his glasses and began cleaning them with a knowing smile on his face. After putting them back on, he said almost spitefully, 'Let's get one thing clear. That's it for you and milling: it's over.'

The doctor asked Huttunen if he'd fought in the wars. On hearing he had, the doctor's eyes lit up with a meaningful gleam. He asked where he had served. Huttunen said that he was in the Karelian Isthmus during the Winter War and north of Ladoga during the last war.

'At the front?'

'Yes . . . men like me were always at the front.'

'Was it tough?'

'Sometimes.'

The doctor jotted something in his notebook. As if to himself, he muttered, 'War neurosis . . . I thought as much.'

Huttunen tried to protest, saying that his nerves had never given him any trouble during the war, and they didn't give him much now, but the doctor waved him out of his office. When Huttunen brought up his leaving again, the doctor looked up from his papers and said, 'These cases of war neurosis are serious, especially when they show up so many years after the actual fighting. It is essential you receive long-term treatment. But I don't want you to worry: we'll make a man out of you.'

Orderlies escorted Huttunen back to his ward. The door banged shut behind him.

The miller wearily sat down on his bed and thought to himself that his life had ground to a complete halt: he was a prisoner of this inhuman institution, at the mercy of the arbitrary decisions of an idiotic doctor, and condemned to the morose company of his unfortunate roommates. He could end up in here for years. Maybe he'd die within these stone walls. From now on a garrulous cleaner and a brutal orderly spoiling for a punch-up would be his only source of distraction. Endless days punctuated solely by supervised trips to the toilets and the pigsty that passed for a dining hall. With a heavy sigh, Huttunen stretched out on his bed and closed his eyes. But sleep wouldn't come. His head felt as if it was being gripped in a vice. He wanted to howl but how could he in front of all these people?

Moments later, Huttunen gave a start: the occupant of the bed near the door had come over on tiptoe.

'Pssst, pretend nothing's happening,' the man said.

Huttunen opened his eyes and looked at him inquiringly.

'I'm not mad but these chappies don't know that,' he continued. 'Let's go and have a chat by the window. You go first, I'll follow in a minute.'

Huttunen went over to the window. His mysterious companion quietly joined him soon afterwards. The man looked outside and then said, as if talking to himself, 'As I said, I'm not mad. And I don't think you've got any more screws loose than I have.'

CHAPTER 13

The man was in his forties, with a broad face and an air of florid good health that was matched by a relaxed, affable manner.

'The name's Happola. But we'd better not shake hands in case the loopy loos see us.'

Huttunen told him he had been a perfectly ordinary miller until a few days before. He had tried to talk to the hospital doctor about getting back to his mill, he said, but the man wouldn't discharge him.

'I'm in property myself,' Happola replied. 'But the war messed up my business when I had to come in here. It is pretty complicated taking care of your affairs from this place. Everything would be much easier if I was free to come and go. But when I've done my ten years in here, I'll stop pretending to be mad. I've got a property in Heinäpää, maybe I'll open a shop or a business.'

His building was rented out for the moment, he said, so his bank account was in pretty good shape. You didn't have any expenses in a hospital.

He had built the property in the Heinäpää district of Oulu in 1938, and had taken on half a dozen tenant families before it was finished. Then the war had broken out and he had been sent to the front. He had skied around Suomussalmi all through the Winter War.

'It was a dangerous time. Many of the men in my company were killed. And that's when I decided that if the fighting ever stopped, I would never go to the front again.'

Between the wars, Happola had brought in new tenants to replace those who had been killed. Business had gone well; Happola had even thought of taking a wife. But with the onset of spring, German soldiers became a common sight on the streets of Oulu, and as spring gave way to summer, the world assumed a more martial air. Happola began thinking of ways to avoid the army if war were to break out again.

'I started limping and complaining of short sight. But the doctor wouldn't sign a medical certificate. Someone had reported I was fit as a fiddle. Of course I didn't always hobble everywhere I went or screw up my eyes every minute of the day.'

Happola wasn't assigned to the softer option of the Territorial Army. Things were looking bad. The business-man's keen nose had scented war.

'That's when I had the idea of pretending to be mad.

At first, people laughed and made fun of me. But I didn't give up. I knew one thing for sure: I wasn't going to fight. It was tough. Not just anybody can pretend to be mad. You have to think it through and be single-minded for people to believe you.'

Interested, Huttunen asked, 'What sort of madness did you fake? Did you start howling?'

'Don't be silly, mad people don't howl . . . I started talking nonsense. I wanted people to think I was paranoid. I said that someone had tried to asphyxiate me in my garage. I suspected doctors of trying to poison me if they gave me medicine. I even wrote to the newspapers. It was mayhem! I reported people left, right and centre to the police, including my bank manager who I said had tried to bankrupt me. That did it. They brought me in here like a shot. And not a moment too soon either: a week later Hitler attacked Russia and a few days after that the Finns followed. But my mess tin wasn't rattling about with all my other kit on my back!'

Having put the building in his sister's name, since he was scared the state would confiscate his assets while he was in its care, Happola had spent the whole war in the asylum. He was soon considered a desperate case. During the war he had put on six pounds.

'In that sense, I was well off here, but time dragged terribly surrounded by the la-las.'

When Finland had pulled out of the war and signed the armistice, Happola had shown signs of recovery. But then the Lapland war had broken out and he had had a relapse. It was only when Germany fell that Happola had fully recovered his faculties. He had asked to return to civilian life just like everyone else.

'They wouldn't let me out, damn it! The doctors patted me on the shoulder: Happola, Happola, let's calm down, shall we?'

The man was resentful. He had always been a perfectly sane native of Oulu, but now no one believed him.

'Why don't you escape?' asked Huttunen.

'Where would I go? You can't hide if you work in property. I have to live in Oulu, since that's where my building is. But you just wait till ten years have passed since the truce. Then this fellow is going straight to the head doctor and telling him the whole story.'

'Why don't you go and tell him now that you have been pretending to be mad all this time?'

'I've often thought about it in the last few years. But it is not that simple. Of course I'd be let out of here, but what would be the good, because I'd just be thrown in jail instead. Pretending to be ill is a crime in wartime, you see, and it only lapses after ten years.'

Huttunen agreed it made sense to wait until he couldn't be prosecuted. It would be tough to go straight from the hospital to prison.

'But how have you run your business from here?' Huttunen asked. 'There are bars on the windows and the doors are locked.'

'I've got my own keys; I bought them a few years ago from an orderly. Still, it's tricky only being able to go in to town in the middle of the night. It is not often I can slip off in the daytime without someone seeing. Once or twice a year, I have to go to collect rent arrears in the day but otherwise I do all my paperwork and stuff at night. It's difficult maintaining a building, especially when people think you're off your trolley.'

'Don't worry. They think I'm off my trolley too,' Huttunen sympathised.

'Well, you must be a bit unhinged. Whereas I've had to pretend to be mad for almost ten years. Everybody else had five years at war, but I've had almost double. It's been hard.'

Happola considered his misfortunes for a moment, but quickly moved on to the more enviable aspects of his situation.

'There is one silver cloud, and that's the money that's been piling up in the bank. You're looked after for free here, you see. I'm going to be pretty well set up when I get out.'

Happola discreetly offered Huttunen a cigarette. He explained that he brought tobacco from town and that sometimes, when time really seemed to drag, he drank a bottle of alcohol under the covers.

'It's not worth trying to get women in here: you get caught immediately. And the ones here are too mad to risk getting them excited.'

They smoked in silence. Huttunen considered Happola's fate. It seemed impossible to escape from this establishment, whether you entered it of your own free will or under duress.

Happola made Huttunen swear that he wouldn't tell anyone his secret. Wouldn't his tenants denounce their landlord when he came to collect his money, Huttunen wondered.

'It's not in their interests to shop me,' Happola replied. 'If they open their mouths, I'll put them out on the street. Luckily there's such a shortage of accommodation in Oulu that that scruffy bunch aren't in a position to say anything anyway. The rent has to be paid on time whether the landlord is mad or not.'

CHAPTER 14

Midsummer at Oulu mental hospital bore little resemblance to the joyous festival of light with which the rest of Finland marked the middle of summer. Admittedly the agitated patients didn't sleep a wink, shouting and rampaging all night, but that wasn't in celebration of the solstice, that was just daily routine. Happola said that the asylum never took much notice of feast days. Only at Christmas did it unbend itself sufficiently to let a small group of Pentecostalists into its innermost recesses where they chanted their saddest dirges. The atmosphere was always pretty oppressive, according to Happola, because the choir were so afraid of the inmates on the locked wards that they shot through their psalms at top speed and, just to be on the safe side, in menacing tones.

'Still, we're not here to have a party,' Happola added sarcastically.

During the week after Midsummer, Huttunen was called to the hospital secretary's office. Two orderlies led him in to see the doctor.

The doctor was immersed in Huttunen's file. Pawing his glasses with his usual ineffectuality, he motioned to the patient to sit down.

'Stand by the door, just in case,' he told the orderlies.

The doctor informed Huttunen that he had studied his file as well as the report submitted by Dr Ervinen from his local medical practice.

'The picture's none too rosy. As I established last time, you appear to have been afflicted by a chronic form of war neurosis. I was a major in the medical corps during the war, so I know this type of complaint very well.'

Huttunen protested. He said there was nothing wrong with him, and asked to leave the hospital. The doctor did not deign to respond, preferring to leaf through a copy of *Military Medicine Review*. Huttunen saw the issue was from 1941. The doctor opened it at the article, 'Some war psychoses and neuroses in wartime and their aftermath'.

'Don't stare. This does not concern you,' the doctor grumbled, cleaning his spectacles. 'These problems have been scientifically studied. It says here that between 1916 and 1918, a third of the English army that fought in the quagmires of Flanders were clinically unfit to fight at the front because of psychoses and neuroses. War psychoses and neuroses have the particularity that they develop very easily among people who suffer from a constitutional infirmity and, having appeared once, they have a propensity to return under the influence of increasingly trifling external events. They also note that in the classes of 1920 to 1939 in the Finnish army, there were between 13,000 and 16,000 people of feeble mind, of which, I presume, the majority took part in the war.'

The doctor looked up, and stared Huttunen in the eye across the table.

'You admitted last time that you took part in both our wars.'

Huttunen nodded but said he didn't see how that proved he was mentally ill.

'I wasn't the only one there.'

The doctor produced further snippets of information from the article for his patient's benefit. The orderlies lit cigarettes to pass the time. Huttunen would have liked to smoke too, but he knew that inmates weren't entitled to even a single drag.

'The mentally subnormal are driven by a primitive instinct of survival in war ... The impulse to surpass oneself and the spirit of sacrifice which were such hallmarks of our army have no hold on them; quite the opposite, they try by every means possible to avoid danger and unpleasant experiences. The case of Sven Dufva in Runeberg* is clearly an extremely rare exception.'

---

* Dufva is one of the heroes of the epic poem *The Tales of Ensign Stål* by Johan Ludvig Runeberg (1804–77), Finland's foremost nineteenth-century poet. Written in Swedish, it details Finnish bravery in the Russo-Swedish war of 1808–09; the first of its tales was adapted to form the Finnish national anthem, 'Maame' ('Our Land').

The doctor gave Huttunen a disgusted look. Then he returned to the article and read a few underlined passages under his breath, before continuing out loud: 'The mentally subnormal react with a state of confusion that is characterised by infantile babbling and problems of perception. The mentally subnormal, in these cases, often soil themselves, smear the walls of their room with their excrement, which they eat, and display other behaviour of this kind . . .'

The doctor turned to the orderlies who were chatting in the doorway to ask if the patient had displayed any of the symptoms in question. The older of the orderlies stubbed out his cigarette in the flowerpot on the windowsill and said, 'As far as I know, he hasn't eaten any shit yet, at any rate.'

Huttunen protested vehemently. It was disgraceful accusing him of such revolting behaviour. He leapt up from his chair in indignation but the two orderlies instantly stood up as well and Huttunen, swallowing his fury, sat back down. The younger of the nurses said casually, 'If you start kicking up a fuss, we'd be better off locking you up, don't you think, Doctor?'

The doctor nodded. He looked sternly at Huttunen.

'Do try and calm down. I can see your nerves are in a bad state.'

If he were free, Huttunen thought to himself, he'd pound these three idiots into the sort of mush they served in the canteen. The doctor carried on quoting from the article, more for his own benefit than that of the orderlies or the patient: 'The shock reactions that appear in the context of violent psychological experiences – bomb and heavy grenade explosions, burial in ruins, hand-to-hand combat – where physical effort is combined with the danger of immediate death, often combine physical and mental symptoms in equal proportion. Among the physical symptoms, one finds problems with sight or hearing, adynamia, and forms of psychogenic paralysis . . . the mental symptoms are distraction, mental block and amnesia, which have the potential to induce a state of total mental confusion. The shock psychosis abates rapidly in most cases, leaving a period of extreme exhaustion, insomnia and a propensity to night terrors. But for many it precipitates a form of nervous reaction that *subsequently* occurs in stressful circumstances.'

The doctor stopped reading. He studied Huttunen attentively and murmured, half to himself, 'Doesn't a mill roar a little like a bomber?'

'It doesn't make that much noise,' Huttunen retorted, exasperated. 'And I wasn't buried under ruins, Doctor, if that's what you're driving at.'

'Shock psychoses are often connected to a cerebral disturbance caused by atmospheric pressure that requires a remarkably long recovery period,' the doctor countered ponderously. 'There can even be permanent after-effects. Whoever has suffered such a reaction is generally incapable of serving at the front, or occupying positions of responsibility. Doesn't the miller's trade involve heavy responsibilities? I imagine one has to deal with everything from the grain to the working of the whole plant.'

Huttunen muttered that the miller's trade was no more demanding than any other line of work. Paying him no particular attention, the doctor read another underlined passage from the article: 'It is relatively common for a person who has fully recovered from a shock reaction to experience a further neurotic reaction on encountering economic difficulties or other setbacks after his release from the army. This fresh neurotic attack must be considered the result of constitutional weakness and circumstances discrete from his military service.'

The doctor put the journal to one side.

'My diagnosis is unequivocal. You are mentally ill: a manic-depressive whose clinical profile includes nervous fragility and neurasthenia. All the result of a war neurosis.'

The doctor paused to clean his spectacles.

'But I do understand. You have clearly had some very gruelling experiences. It says in this report that you had a habit of howling, especially in winter and at night. And that you used to impersonate animals . . . We still have to get to the bottom of all this, particularly this tendency to howl. I have not come across many patients in my career who have been strongly inclined to howl. Most have simply whimpered and moaned.'

The doctor asked the orderlies if the patient had howled since he had been in the hospital.

'Not that we've heard. But we'll come and tell you if he starts.'

'Let him howl. It's not as if there isn't any noise in here already.'

Turning to Huttunen, the doctor remarked, 'As you've just heard, you have special permission to howl in this hospital. I would prefer it, however, if you refrain from doing so at night. It could agitate the other patients.'

'I won't howl here,' Huttunen said bitterly.

'You can bay absolutely as you please. I am of the school that thinks one can learn a great deal about a patient's condition by the types of sounds he makes.'

'I'm not howling. I don't want to.'

The doctor tried to sway him.

'Couldn't you emit a little howl now, just so I can see? It would be interesting to hear how you howl when the mood takes you.'

Huttunen calmly said that he wasn't insane; he was just a bit odd at most. In any case, the way things were nowadays, you came across much stranger people than him the whole time. The doctor had resumed polishing his glasses. Vexed, Huttuned added, 'I think those goggles must be clean by now. Do you really have to rub them the whole time?'

The doctor hurriedly put his glasses back on.

'It's a harmless habit, a form of repetitive behaviour. You wouldn't understand.'

He motioned to the orderlies to remove the patient. They grabbed Huttunen by both arms and dragged him into the corridor, kicking him in the small of the back to make him hurry up. In the ward, they forced him to lie down on his bed. Then the door slammed and the key turned furiously in the lock.

CHAPTER 15

Over the next few days, Huttunen realised that he was not going to be let out of the asylum immediately, or perhaps even ever. He tried to talk to the doctor again but the man refused to see him, instead prescribing drugs that the brawny orderly forced Huttunen to take.

Huttunen thought of his red mill on the Suukoski rapids, and of Sanelma Käyrämö, and of the beautiful summer that he could now only glimpse through the bars on the window now. He felt excruciatingly bad. He tried to talk to his companions but, in their confusions, they couldn't understand a word he was saying; Happola was the only one he could have a whispered conversation with from time to time.

Days passed. Huttunen's anguish intensified. He stayed lying on his bed all day, turned in on himself, meditating on the wretched turn his life had taken. He stared at the bars on the window: they cut him off from the rest of the world, with cold, inescapable finality. They were too strong to bend and the door was permanently locked. Huttunen tried to see if there was any way to get out from the dining room but there were always muscular orderlies on duty. Not a hope. Huttunen imagined that, if the worst came to the worst, he wouldn't walk out of this establishment on his own two feet; he'd just be shipped off to the morgue where a pathologist would chop up his body with an axe into suitably sized pieces for medical research.

Sometimes at night Huttunen was overcome by an anguish and horror so intense that he had to get up and walk about the twilit room for hours, pacing back and forth like an animal in a zoo. Huttunen felt like a prisoner who hadn't committed a crime and had been sentenced without trial. He had nothing: no rights, no obligations, no choices. All he had were his thoughts and his wild craving for freedom that he had no way of appeasing. Huttunen felt he was going mad in that room surrounded by apathetic, suffering inmates.

One day the skinny lad who grimaced non-stop made another attempt to tell Huttunen about his life. The narrative was so confused that he had a lot of trouble following it.

It was a dreadful story. The wretched boy was the son of a mentally unstable, unmarried mother. He had been hungry and maltreated for as long as he could remember. When his mother was sent to prison – who knows what for – the boy was auctioned off to a family of alcoholics where he had to work non-stop for a boss who drank and a bunch of half-witted farmhands, and as he was a puny lad, he had to endure the cruellest mockery on top of his other humiliations. He was not allowed to go to school, or even hospital, despite having dysentery, typhoid fever and pneumonia at least twice. And then, when at the age of fifteen he had stolen a bit of bacon from the larder, the farmer had taken him to court and the boy had found himself in prison. In his cell he had been beaten for a year by a disgusting multiple murderer. When he finally came out of prison, he had hidden in isolated barns for an entire summer, living mainly off berries, ants' eggs and frogs. In autumn, the barns had been used to store hay and the boy had been caught, but, instead of being taken back to prison, had been brought to the hospital. Since then everything had been going relatively OK.

The scrawny tyke wept. Huttunen tried to console him but the young lad couldn't restrain his tears. Huttunen felt even sadder than before. How could life be so horrendously painful, he wondered.

The little fellow, however, soon forgot the whole story, and went back and sat on his bed, a stream of joyful, uncertain and fearful expressions again playing by turns across his face. Huttunen drew his blanket over his head and thought he really was going mad.

The two following nights, Huttunen didn't sleep at all. He didn't eat; he didn't even get out of bed. When Happola furtively offered him a cigarette on the second evening, the miller turned to face the wall. What the devil did he want with a cigarette when he couldn't get to sleep and food made him want to throw up?

That night, Huttunen paced round the room again. The other patients were snoring in their sleep. The sombre pair at the end of the room farted from time to time. The skinny lad moaned softly, crying, the poor boy, in his sleep. Huttunen's head ached; his temples throbbed. His throat was dry; his mind had ground to a complete standstill.

He began to whine very quietly. The sound welled up in his throat, plaintive, muffled; it grew a little stronger, and then suddenly Huttunen let out such a powerful howl that all the occupants of the room flew out of their beds and huddled against the back wall.

Huttunen howled with all his might, venting all his sorrow, his hunger for freedom, his loneliness and anguish. The room's stone walls seemed to crack open under the violence of his cry, the iron beds to vibrate at the power of his voice. The light in the ceiling flickered, and then came on. Three orderlies rushed into the room and led Huttunen to his bed. The frame squeaked as they sat on the miller's back to reduce him to silence.

When the orderlies had left and the light had been switched off, Happola came over to Huttunen's bed and whispered, 'Christ almighty, that scared me.'

'I won't last in here any longer,' Huttunen said wearily. 'Lend me that key, I'm going.'

Happola understood, but nonetheless observed that escaping wouldn't do much good: the hospital would just have him brought back. But Huttunen was adamant.

'If I don't get out of here soon, I'm going to lose my mind.'

Happola agreed. He knew all too well how painful it was being locked up in hospital when you wanted to get out.

They made arrangements that night. Happola's business-man's instincts would not allow him to organise the escape without some form of compensation. He said it would cost six sacks of barley flour. Huttunen thought that was a fair price.

'Send the sacks to Oulu station when you've got your business going,' Happola said. 'There's no hurry, but fair's fair. I had to pay for the keys myself. And anyway, I've never got anyone out of here for free.'

Happola told how three years earlier he had helped a patient escape who, once a free woman, had become the most sought-after prostitute on the whole coast of the Gulf of Bothnia.

'She was very pretty. A bit agitated, perhaps. Now she lives in Oulu but she works in Raahe and Kokkala, and even goes as far afield as Pori. I got a good price for that key. So don't forget to send me that flour.'

Happola had business to see to in town in a couple of days, so that would be Huttunen's chance to escape from the asylum.

Once the institution was plunged in sleep, Happola opened the door of the ward with his key. The men slipped noiselessly through the long, silent corridors of the huge hospital to the kitchen and adjoining laundry. In the laundry's storeroom, they found Huttunen's clothes in a box alongside the other patients' belongings. Huttunen's was on top of the first row; he was one of the most recent arrivals, after all. He put on his clothes, did up his belt and checked his wallet. Some of his money had been taken but, oddly enough, not all. Huttunen folded the pyjama suit, cap and slippers away in the box and then put it back in its place.

'You don't get changed!' Huttunen exclaimed in surprise as his companion strolled along the corridor in his pyjamas.

'No need in summer. If I've got to go into town during the day, that's different. I've got a stylish two-piece in the cupboard in the laundry, but there's no need to wear a suit for these night trips. It would just get crumpled for nothing.'

The men went out of a side door and crossed the garden by a crunching gravel path. They climbed a hill planted with pines to an old red-brick water tower. Huttunen turned round. The sombre, looming asylum building lay in the small valley. Not a light shone in its windows; no one was pursuing the fugitives. Escaping that house of horrors had been incredibly easy.

A monotonous moaning rose up from the gabled window of the women's wing. One of the agitated patients was bewailing her lot.

Huttunen shivered at the inconsolable lament. He wanted to howl back, to answer in his fashion the call of this unfortunate woman whom unknown sufferings had driven to groan so piteously.

Huttunen was about to raise a booming howl to the heavens, when Happola said in a quiet voice, 'Liisa Kastikainen. She'll have been talking for three years soon. Three years exactly in the autumn. I still remember when they brought her in. She was tied up in blankets. At the start they tried to make her wear a wooden gag, but the clinical director banned it when she left her dentures in it.'

At the foot of the water tower a road led to town. In the luminous summer night, the men set off in silence towards Oulu, the White City of the North.

CHAPTER 16

At Heinäpää, they found Happola's one-storey wooden house. The paint had flaked away during the war but otherwise it was in good condition. Recognising Happola, the dog in the yard wagged enthusiastically at Huttunen as well. Happola chose a key from a big bunch. On the steps, he exclaimed, 'What do you reckon? For someone who's meant to be a few bricks short of a load, I've got a pretty good place, eh? The mortgage is paid off and I've got money in the bank. I could pay cash for a new car if I had a licence. I applied to import one privately in fact, but they said I was certified.'

There were several doors leading off the hallway, each with a different name.

'My tenants . . . there's more upstairs.'

Happola opened one of the doors. It gave onto a room

with two beds, a table and a few chairs. A middle-aged woman was asleep in one of the beds.

'It's you . . . Am I on again?' she asked in a sleepy voice.

'No need to get undressed,' Happola said. 'I just bought a friend over for a moment. Give him something to eat tomorrow morning, but otherwise leave him be.'

The woman lay back down and quickly fell asleep. Happola started making plans for Huttunen's future.

'If I were you, I'd sell the mill and go to America. If the States won't have you, you should shoot off to Spain. A major I know went there after the wars and apparently he loves it. He earns his living growing carnations. Have you got much land with your mill?'

'Only a few acres,' Huttunen replied, 'but the mill's in good shape and there's a shingle saw that's almost brand new. I even had time to repaint it before they took me away. It has two stones, one for flour and one for animal feed. You just have to start it up. The top of the millrace is all new and the bottom has been repaired. You'll be able to mill with it for years without it needing any work.'

Happola made a few telephone calls to different parts of the province offering Huttunen's mill for sale, but he didn't find any takers.

'It's pretty difficult doing business in the middle of the night,' Happola said. 'Everyone in property seems to be asleep. I'll have to come back the day after tomorrow and make some more calls in the day; I know someone in Kajaani who might be interested. But I've got to go now.

I'll have to be in my bed tomorrow morning when they find out you've escaped.'

Happola gave Huttunen a farewell cigarette and slipped silently out the door. The miller looked around the room: it had dirty wallpaper, a couple of rag rugs, and a corner stove that smoked, judging by the grimy streaks above the door. On the bedside table, there were curlers and a set of dentures in a glass of water.

Huttunen undressed and got into the second bed. Then he got up to turn off the light. He wanted to pee, but didn't dare wake the woman to ask here where the toilet was. Despite his discomfort, he slept until morning.

Huttunen was woken by the sound of running water. His bladder instantly felt even closer to bursting. The light was on but the woman wasn't in the room. Huttunen got dressed and stood impatiently waiting for her to come out of the toilet. When she reappeared, he stormed past her so quickly he didn't have time to say good morning.

The woman made some coffee, which she put on the table with slices of bread and butter, and some little raisin buns. Huttunen told her that he'd escaped from the bin.

'Me too,' the woman replied. 'Happola got me out. He hasn't left me in peace since. He comes and has a cuddle twice a week.'

The woman had combed her hair, and put on lipstick and earrings. She was wearing a skin-tight red skirt and a white ruched blouse. Her figure was soft and plump. She explained that she'd had to become a prostitute to make a living; Happola had asked such a high price for the keys and the rent, that otherwise she would have ended up back in the asylum.

'Better to be a hooker and free than locked up in the nuthouse. It'll be time to go back when no one wants me anymore. I am still pretty crazy.'

Huttunen thanked her for the coffee and got up to leave.

'Are you going to go without having sex, now you know what I do?' the woman asked in amazement.

Thrown, Huttunen bowed in the doorway and then rushed out. Once in the street, he was overwhelmed by memories of the horticulture adviser Sanelma Käyrämö: the cool shade under the mosquito net; the fragrant hay; the stillness of Leppäsaari Island; her sweet voice; the gentle touch of her hand; the way her hair tickled as it brushed his nose. Huttunen set off for the station, buying a postcard and stamp on the way.

Huttunen took a train north. Oulu, city of evil memory, fell away behind him. Once the train had crossed the Tuira bridges, he took out the postcard and addressed it to the mental hospital.

Dear Doctor,

I have escaped from your madhouse. Perhaps you've already noticed. I'm going to Sweden and then Norway, so just leave me in peace. Anyway, I wasn't mad in the first place. I'll leave you to get on with cleaning your specs.

Huttunen

* * *

At Kemi, Huttunen dropped the card in the station letterbox. He smiled at the thought of them looking for him in Sweden and Norway. Before the train pulled out, he bought a dozen hard-boiled eggs at the station buffet. When they reached the village, he avoided the road leading to the centre, and cut through the woods straight to the Suukoski rapids.

The miller gave himself up to the joy of homecoming. The beautiful red mill stood proudly in its place in the summer sun. Huttunen checked the dam, the millrace, the shingle saw and the turbine. Everything was fine. All nature seemed to be celebrating his return; the stream babbled gaily under the mill like a cheerful friend.

The mill door was boarded up. Huttunen tore it open, sending nails and planks flying into the grass.

It was a mess inside. His things had been searched, his bed was rumpled, the sideboard door had been torn off, saucepans were missing. The cupboard had been emptied of everything edible. Even the sack of potatoes Huttunen had left right at the back had disappeared.

His rifle wasn't on the wall anymore. Had the police chief come and confiscated it or had it been stolen? There wasn't a crust of bread in the store cupboard. To stave off his hunger, Huttunen swallowed the last of the eggs he'd bought at Kemi and washed them down with a ladle of water.

He went through his belongings and realised to his fury how much was missing: a trunk, his Sunday suit, his rifle, some tools, a pot, a sheet, a flowery pillowcase, all the food . . . Huttunen threw himself on his bed, sickened, trying to work out who could have been responsible for the pillage. Suddenly he leapt to his feet, strode over to the corner of the room and got down on his knees by the wall; he lifted up the outer floorboard and thrust his hand into the lagging. He searched up and down, groping around in the sawdust. The miller's face tensed, and then grew more and more desperate, until at last it lit up jubilantly. With a yell, he bounded back to the centre of the room in a single stride, a savings book clasped in his hand.

Huttunen let out an awesome howl, just like the good old days. The sound of his own voice frightened him, and he crept over to the window to see if anyone had heard. There was no one in sight; the miller felt calmer. He shook the sawdust off the savings book. According to the balance, he still had money in his account. In every other respect, his affairs had come to a complete dead end.

Huttunen went to the window to look at his vegetable garden that had started to turn green during his stay in Oulu. It was clear that someone had been taking care of it: there wasn't a single weed growing among the vegetable shoots, the rows were carefully hoed and thinned. The horticulture adviser Sanelma Käyrämö must have been tending his patch in his absence, he guessed.

Delirious with happiness, he ran outside and minutely scrutinised the garden. Between the rows, he found the imprint of a small woman's foot.

Thank God for vegetables.

CHAPTER 17

Huttunen gazed longingly out of the mill window at his vegetable patch for two days, yearning with all his heart for the horticulture adviser Sanelma Käyrämö to come riding down the hill on her bicycle and start bustling about among the vegetables.

But he waited in vain. The adviser didn't come, and in his disappointment, Huttunen thought it was actually pretty irresponsible to leave a vegetable garden untended for so long.

It had been a while now since the miller had had a proper meal. He remembered the thick hospital mush at Oulu that he'd reluctantly forced down. Now just thinking about that wretched food made his mouth water. And what about the eggs he'd bought at Kemi station! Huttunen could have eaten a basket in one go. He had to make do with water for the time being. As a side dish, he scraped

up a few handfuls of last year's flour from the cracks
between the floorboards. But this hardly stilled his hunger,
especially because it had a disgusting amount of dust
mixed in with it.

On the evening of the second day, hunger finally drove
the miller out of the mill. He crept down to the ground
floor, lifted the trapdoor leading to the turbine house and
stole outside. He headed through the woods to Tervola's
shop. He was so hungry he could barely see where he
was going; in the willows on the riverbank, branches struck
him in the face, his eyes filled with tears and he felt a
lump in his throat, a lump of sadness and starvation,
rather than food.

Huttunen hid for a long while in the bushes by the
shop, watching to see if any villagers were doing their
shopping or hanging around nearby. When he was sure
that the shopkeeper and his wife were alone, he knocked
on the back door. Tervola came to open it. Recognising
his visitor, he tried to jam the door shut, but Huttunen
managed to get his foot in the crack.

'You can't come in, Kunnari. We're closed.'

Huttunen asked to speak to the shopkeeper alone.
Grudgingly, Tervola ushered him into the shop, leaving
the door open so that his wife could hear them. Huttunen
sat on some sacks of potatoes, took a bottle of beer out
of a crate and began drinking slowly. Then he ran through
his shopping list.

'I'll have some ordinary sausage, a pound, a pound of
bacon, a pound of butter as well, two packets of cigarettes

– Työkansas – coffee, sugar, half a bushel of spuds, some tobacco.'

'I don't serve lunatics.'

Huttunen took money out of his purse.

'I'll pay double if I have to, but give me the food, I'm dying of hunger.'

'I've already told you we're closed. I won't sell you anything; you should've stayed at Oulu. You're a criminal on the run.'

Tervola paused for a moment, thinking, and then went on, 'It was so peaceful when you weren't here. The whole village was happy. The best thing you can do is go away. I'm not going to sell you a thing.'

Huttunen put the empty bottle of beer back in the crate and tossed a couple of coins on the counter. Then he said calmly, 'I'm not leaving here without any food. For God's sake, the last time I ate was Thursday, or even Wednesday, at Oulu.'

Shaking his head, Tervola retreated behind the counter. But when Huttunen took a step towards him, he began hurriedly piling up food on the counter. He yanked sugar and coffee off the shelves, grabbed salt fish, bacon and butter, scooped up flour and potatoes from their bins. He stacked this mass of food in front of Huttunen, slamming the bags and packets onto the counter's glass top hard enough to make the windows tremble. On top of the pile, he chucked a few packets of tobacco and ten big boxes of matches.

'Take it! Steal it!'

Huttunen held out money but Tervola didn't want it.

'Steal it! Have it all! I won't take your money but you can steal from me if you must. What chance has an old man like me against a maniac like you?'

Huttunen had already started gathering up his supplies. He put the packets back on the counter, shouting, 'I have never stolen a thing in my life and I'm not going to start now. My money's as good as anybody's.'

But the shopkeeper didn't want his money. He brushed aside the notes the miller repeatedly tried to put in his hand. Then he measured out two pounds of wheat semolina and a pound of dried raisins into bags, slung those on the counter and barked, 'Steal those too!'

Huttunen couldn't stand this treatment any longer. He rushed out of the front door of the shop, which was locked. A shower of rivets tinkled on the hall floor in his wake.

Tervola went out onto the porch to see where the miller had run off to. There was no one in sight, but a noise was coming from the woods. The shopkeeper assumed it was Huttunen. He went back into his shop and quickly put everything lying on the counter back where it belonged. Then he went into his flat to telephone the police.

The shopkeeper Tervola told Constable Portimo that Huttunen had escaped from the bin. The fugitive had come into his shop and tried to buy food with force, but Tervola had refused to sell him anything.

'Kunnari had money. But I was not for turning and wouldn't take a penny. He has just run off into the woods, so you'd better find him and arrest him. Otherwise the howling's going to start again.'

When the conversation was over, Constable Portimo donned his official cap with a sigh and set off on his bicycle towards the Suukoski rapids.

Huttunen sat in the mill house, his stomach empty, his head in his hands. It was already late in the evening. Soon the lonely, starving night would fall. The miller drank water from the ladle and wearily went back to the window. If only the horticulture adviser Sanelma Käyrämö would come down the hill on her bicycle, things might take a turn for the better.

But it was an old man who appeared on the hill, a man who Huttunen recognised as Constable Portimo.

CHAPTER 18

The police constable left his bicycle against the wall of the mill and made a noisy entrance. He saw that the boards nailed across the door had been pulled off, which meant there was every likelihood the miller was at home, and called up the stairs in a conciliatory voice, 'It's only the police, Huttunen, don't worry!'

Huttunen offered Portimo a seat. The police constable gave the miller a cigarette. It was the first he'd smoked in a long time. Inhaling deeply, he said, 'They even took my cigarettes at Oulu.'

Portimo asked if Oulu had let Huttunen out. In a low voice, Huttunen admitted, 'I ran away.'

'That's what Tervola suspected when he rang. How about if you come along with me now?'

'I wouldn't come even if you shot me on the spot.'

The police constable calmed him down, assuring him there wasn't any question of shooting. The shopkeeper had telephoned, that was all. Huttunen asked if the police chief had been told about his escape. Portimo said that Oulu hadn't sent through a request, and the police chief didn't know the miller was back in the canton yet.

'So why have you come to arrest me if you haven't been given any orders?'

Portimo admitted that no, it was true, he didn't have any orders. But as the shopkeeper had called . . .

'The thing is, I have been running a tab with Tervola for three months. I sort of have to do what he says. You can't afford to upset a grocer on a police constable's salary. I've got my son at Jyväskylä studying education; he wants to become a teacher. It's expensive, you know, bringing up a boy. Do you remember Antero? He spent whole summers at the mill listening to you. The lad with long legs.'

'Oh, that one . . . But look, talking of something else . . . I'm terribly hungry. I couldn't get any food at the shop, and it wasn't for lack of money. I can tell you. It's almost three days since I had a proper meal and that was only that bloody slop. Believe me, I am absolutely bloody starving.'

Portimo promised to discuss the question of food with his wife, but they couldn't do something every day, and they wouldn't bring things to the mill. Maybe there was somewhere they could meet in the forest, say.

'A policeman has to be careful when he's helping a wanted man. I wouldn't give a criminal food, but it's a bit different with you. And I know you as well, anyway.'

Portimo gave him another cigarette.

'Listen Kunnari, wouldn't it be more sensible to sell up and go to America? From what I've heard, madness isn't such a big thing over there; mad people are free to walk around as they please. As long as you did your work, you wouldn't be harassed.'

'I don't understand a word of English and I don't speak any either. I can't even go to Sweden: I don't know the language and it takes a long time to pick it up at my age.'

'That's true . . . but you can't stay in the mill. We'd get a wanted person description tomorrow if you did, and then I'd be forced to arrest you and take you back to Oulu. The police have to obey the law as well, you know.'

'Where can I go?'

Portimo started thinking. What if Huttunen went into the woods? It was summer; the good weather had well and truly arrived. The miller could live in the forest to start with, try to sell the mill through someone, and then discreetly leave the country.

'You just have to take a phrase book and study in the wild. Once you've learnt the language and the mill's been sold, all you have to do is nip over to Sweden through the woods, across the Torniojoki, and the world's at your feet.'

Huttunen considered the plan. It was true that he couldn't stay at the mill any longer. But escaping into the woods was a daunting prospect. How would he get by?

'Think of the "armies of the forest", those deserters who lived in the woods, some for years,' Portimo exclaimed enthusiastically. 'You can survive in the forest just as well as any traitor to this country. And if you get caught, there won't be a military tribunal to have you shot. There'll just be a little drive to Oulu.'

As the men talked, evening gave way to night. Portimo sat at the window, keeping a lookout so that no one could take them by surprise. Everything was quiet.

Huttunen asked who had cleaned out his store cupboard and taken his tools. Portimo said he had come with the police chief to confiscate the rifle and axe for reasons of public safety. The pastoress had taken the food and given it to the needy of the parish.

'She didn't have to take the sack of potatoes. The spuds wouldn't have gone off in the cupboard.'

'I don't know about the potatoes. Perhaps they thought you'd be in Oulu for years.'

'My God, to think that I had to lick flour off the floor! Life can be complete hell if you're mad. And I'm not even properly mad. There were some really mad people at Oulu.'

Portimo gave a start and pointed out of the window, 'Look, Kunnari ... Look who's bending down in the vegetable garden!'

Huttunen rushed to the window, tipping over his chair. Someone was bustling around in his vegetable patch, a woman. Huttunen instantly recognised the horticulture adviser Sanelma Käyrämö, crouching at the edge of a row of beetroot, pulling out weeds. Huttunen tore out of the mill, taking the steps five at a time.

Portimo saw the miller leap over the bed of turnips, grab the adviser in his arms and give her a smacking kiss. Once her initial fright had passed, the horticulturist recognised the apparition and threw herself into his arms, wrapping herself around him and hugging him as tight as she could.

After a while, when the sound of animated conversation rose up from the vegetable patch, Portimo opened the window and shouted out to the couple, 'Be quiet! Someone might hear you and take it upon themselves to call the police! Come in here!'

The horticulture adviser and the miller climbed up to the mill house, radiant with happiness. They remained silent for a long time until, with a cough, the police constable observed, 'Our Kunnari's affairs are not looking too healthy. What do you think, as a counsellor?'

The horticulture adviser simply nodded, intimidated by the policeman's gaze. Portimo continued, 'Kunnari and I were thinking that perhaps he should nip off into the woods. At least until autumn. We could see how it went.'

The adviser agreed once more and looked at Huttunen, who seemed to be of the same mind. Portimo sought to adopt a more administrative tone: 'How about if we, that is the counsellor and I, agree that we don't officially know anything about this man? It's a bit tricky for public servants to help a fellow in his situation . . . I mean, we should keep it secret that we're helping him.'

They agreed on this, and also that the horticulture adviser would bring Huttunen food from Portimo's wife that night.

The three of them left the mill together. Huttunen took a blanket and a raincoat and put on a pair of gumboots.

On the road, Portimo solemnly held out his hand to Huttunen.

'Try to make the best of it, Kunnari. Circumstances are to blame here, not people. Trust me, I have no intention of coming looking for you.'

When Portimo had left, the miller and the horticulture adviser went to Leppäsaari Island, with Sanelma Käyrämö making a detour to pick up some potatoes and gravy in a lunch box from Portimo's. The food got a little cold on the way, but it was just what the starving miller needed. He ate in silence, almost reverently. His large Adam's apple bobbed up and down. The horticulture adviser found this so touching that she put one hand on his shoulder and stroked his hair with the other. Had grey hairs appeared since the last time they'd seen each other? In the half-light of the tent, it was impossible to be sure.

The horticulture adviser rinsed out the lunch box in the stream. Huttunen walked her back to the edge of the island, but didn't follow her over to the other side. Tears filled his eyes as the woman disappeared into the trees.

Huttunen went dejectedly back to his tent, lay down on the dried hay and thought that he was alone now. The night was completely silent, with not a trace of birdsong.

PART TWO

The hermit at bay

CHAPTER 19

Gunnar Huttunen's life had reached an ominous pass: he was now no more than a miller without a mill, a man without a home. Having been cast out by humans, he had now in turn cast himself out from their society. Who knew how long he'd have to shun their haunts.

Sitting on the edge of the stream, Huttunen listened to the song of the water racing down from its distant spring in the cool summer night. If he'd had a tumour in his chest, they would have left him in peace, he thought. He would have been pitied and supported and allowed to face his illness amidst his fellow men. But just because his mind worked differently to other people's, he was beyond the pale, he had to be banished from the social order. Still, he preferred this seclusion to the bars on the hospital windows, with only poor melancholy wretches for company.

A trout or grayling jumped in the shadowy river. Huttunen started; the ring floated past, breaking up and melting back into the stream. The thought occurred to him that he wouldn't be eating any more bread or bacon as he had as a miller. It was strictly fish and game from now on.

Huttunen put his hand in the cool water and imagined himself as a brook trout, one weighing a couple of pounds at least. He pictured himself swimming upstream, against the current, rippling and darting between the stones in the shallow water, resting for a moment in the lee of a moss-covered rock, working his fins, opening his gills, breaking the surface of the water with his mouth and then instantly diving back down and gliding away with a flick of his tail. The rushing water rang in his head as he swam further upstream into the night. But the desire for a cigarette soon brought him back to the present; forgetting about the fish for the moment, he resumed thinking about his life.

One thing frightened him: mightn't a hermit's life make him go completely mad? If he looked in the same direction for too long it felt as if an iron band was gripping his forehead. He had to shake his head violently from side to side to relieve the pressure.

Huttunen got to his feet, broke a few alder branches without knowing why, threw them in the stream and muttered, 'If it's like this, I could easily go out of my mind.'

Sunk in thought, he returned to his tent. Notions, each more bizarre than the last, flashed through his mind, making it impossible for him to sleep. It was only when the first birds of the morning began singing that Huttunen drifted off for a few moments, assailed by such oppressive dreams that he woke up drenched in a cold sweat.

Huttunen washed in the stream that, although the sun was already up, still had its dawn chill. He was hungry again, and yet, even after such a short sleep, he felt better, full of energy and verve. His brain was teeming with plans for his hermit's life.

The adviser would bring him food at first, but Huttunen realised that she wouldn't be able to support a man of his size in the woods on her meagre salary for long. He made a list of objects that would help him survive on his own in the forest: an axe, a hunting knife, a rucksack, kitchen implements, clothes . . . There was no end to it. The hermit decided to go to the Suukoski rapids to kit himself out. It was still so early that no one would have come looking for him yet at the mill. He ran through the woods to the rapids, slipped under the mill into the turbine house and, from there, through the trapdoor into the building and up to his room.

Huttunen took his relatively new rucksack out of the cupboard. It was a stroke of luck he'd bought it. During the war, particularly the retreat, Huttunen had cursed his miserable army rucksack that had carried almost nothing but had been incredibly heavy and always full, whacking him in the small of the back, and chafing and cutting into his shoulders, especially when he had to run. This one was big and sturdy, its broad straps were padded with thick felt and it had a belt and all sorts of straps and webbing to hang things from. It looked like the harness and saddle combined of a small horse. Huttunen set about filling it.

A saucepan, a kettle, a frying pan, a cup, a spoon, a fork. What else? Huttunen stuffed two little jars of salt and sugar into the rucksack's pockets, along with some camphor and iodine drops and paregoric powder, which, as it happened, was all the medicine there was in the mill.

The hermit tightly rolled up his fur cap and tucked it inside a blanket. He cut on old flannel shirt into strips to bind his feet, two at the front and two at the back. With the woollen socks he was wearing that should be enough. His gumboots were luckily in good nick, but he'd better take some puncture repair patches anyway. He examined the boots' leather soles admiringly: he never scuffed his feet when he was walking, he wasn't in the slightest bow-legged, and that saved boots a lot of wear. Some people who don't run anywhere get through two pairs of boots a year just because of the rubbing.

A whetstone and a file . . .

Huttunen thrust them to the bottom of a pocket. He fetched a saw from the woodshed, removed its frame, rolled up the blade, wrapped it in paper and tied it to the rucksack. Then he went out to get the clothesline. There wouldn't be much washing hung out on the hill by Suukoski mill in the near future.

A handful of three-inch nails. A comb, a mirror, a razor, a shaving brush and some soap. A pencil and a notebook with blue squared paper. What didn't he need? Should he pack some books? Huttunen realised he had read his entire collection several times over; there was no point lugging them around the depths of the forest. The radio? Too heavy. He might be able to carry the set on its own through the brushwood, but you couldn't carry it with the battery.

He flicked it on. It was the morning news; they were talking about the Korean War. They just had to bring it up every day, didn't they, Huttunen thought to himself. Of course these yokels loved the Korean War: plenty had got rich selling timber since it had sent prices soaring. A farmer didn't need a massive log pile or stack of timber nowadays to be able to treat himself to a tractor. In the spring, Vittavaara and Siponen had sold such a mountain of lumber that they'd be comfortable for years. Irritated, Huttunen switched off the radio.

And that damn Mrs Siponen dares stay in bed claiming she's paralysed. I won't give Siponen a penny for his wife.

He needed a needle and thread and some buttons as well. He tore the North Finland page out of his old school atlas. Pity he didn't have a compass. Two pairs of underwear and some long johns. Mittens and felt slippers. The fur cap was in already. Huttunen rolled up his sheepskin-lined leather jacket and tied it on top of the rucksack.

Who knows if I won't have to hide out in the woods all winter . . . this was an expensive jacket when I bought it in Kokkola after the war.

A plane, a chisel, a pick, and a one-inch diameter drill bit. Any kind of wood would do for a handle. But he wondered whether a plane would be useful in the forest. Better to leave it? He thought that if he had to stay in the wild until winter, he would need skis. He wasn't going to take his own now. He imagined himself wandering along with a pair of skis over his shoulder in the middle of summer.

If anyone saw me, they'd think I was mad.

Huttunen stuffed the plane into his rucksack. A candle. Matches. Binoculars: one of the lenses had been blurred since they had fallen into the Svir during the war, but you could see very well with the other; he'd finally have time to take them apart and clean them. Scissors. Fishing tackle: nets, a dozen spinners and daps, line, hooks, swivels, a piece of lead. He was going to have to get his food with this from now on; at least he had what he needed. He had plenty of flies as well, having tied swarms of them all last winter.

The rucksack was so full that it was tricky actually getting it on his back. Huttunen tested the weight. He was almost doubled over for a minute and unable to stand up.

Huttunen dragged the rucksack down from his room, through the trapdoor and out into the wood behind the river. He broke into a thick sweat hefting such a heavy load at the double. Hiding it among the firs, he went back to the mill, because it had occurred to him that a zinc bucket might be useful in his hideout. A bit cumbersome, but not too heavy.

Bucket in hand, Huttunen tried to think of anything he might have forgotten. He seemed to have everything.

He was just looking out the window at the vegetable garden, thinking that maybe he should take a few turnips – they were big enough to eat – when he saw a group of men at the edge of the plantation. A dozen villagers were standing in a circle around the police chief. The miller realised they had come looking for him. In a trice, he was running downstairs. The bucket banged against the doorframe; Huttunen was afraid they'd hear outside. He opened the trapdoor and slipped down into the turbine house. Just as he did so, the door of the mill crashed open and the men burst in. Huttunen recognised Constable Portimo's voice saying, 'There was no one here yesterday, at any rate. Perhaps he ran off into the woods.'

The men walked over Huttunen's head; the trapdoor creaked. Flour dust trickled down between the floorboards. The miller was painfully crouched over in the narrow pen, praying no one started up the mill. He would be done for otherwise: the turbine blades would grind him to a pulp in that tiny space. From the upstream wall water dripped down his neck; it must have run off from the millrace. The miller found himself thinking that he would have to seal it in the autumn.

He made out the voices of Vittavaara, Siponen, the shopkeeper Tervola, the police constable and the police chief. There were two other men as well, possibly the schoolteacher and Launola, Siponen's farmhand. 'He's been here,' he heard Vittavaara say. 'Look how neatly swept the floor is.'

The men went up the stairs, calling Huttunen. The police chief yelled up from the bottom that resistance was pointless.

'Come out peacefully. You don't stand a chance against us!'

The men soon established that the room at the top of the mill was empty. Annoyed, they came back down the stairs. 'Whatever else you say,' Vittavaara observed, 'he did do a good job fixing up the mill before he went mad.'

All of them went out except for the fat farmer, who had apparently engaged the driving belt. Huttunen heard the clacking of the millstones. Vittavaara shouted to the others outside, 'How about we get the mill turning to have a look? Who knows, it might revert to the commune in the autumn. We could mill our own grain.'

Huttunen was panic stricken. If they started up the mill, he'd be crushed to death. It wasn't a difficult thing to do: they just had to close the gate over the shingle saw, the seething water would come flooding into the turbine house, and the turbine would inexorably start to turn. They'd hear the zinc bucket crumpling first, then the sound of bone being crushed.

Huttunen gripped the blades of the waterwheel as hard as he could, wedged the bucket against his chest and flattened it into an oval. He resolved that if the turbine started turning, he would fight it for all his worth. He calculated how much horsepower it would generate given the water flow in the middle of summer. It was going to take an insane amount of strength to stay alive.

He could hear the police chief outside shouting that now wasn't the moment to get the madman's mill turning. But someone had had time to reach the sluice gate over the shingle saw and, from the lapping sound, Huttunen guessed that they had closed it. The first cascade of water shot into the turbine house, soaking him from head to foot. He bent back the turbine blades with all his strength. Everything went black. Put up a hell of a fight, he told himself: life or death. The water came rushing full bore down the channel, almost drowning Huttunen, yet he shook himself and held firm. The huge volume of water pressed down on the wheel to turn it, but Huttunen wouldn't let it move an inch. A taste of bile filled his mouth; the blood vessels in his head felt as if they were going to burst. Still he didn't let go. Giving in to the water now would have meant relinquishing any claim on life.

'It's not turning,' Vittavaara shouted from the mill. 'The bloody thing's stuck.'

There were answering shouts outside that Huttunen didn't understand. Then the flow of water slowed and soon came to a complete halt. Someone had opened the sluice gate over the shingle saw. Dripping with water, Huttunen realised he had outmatched his mill for strength. His whole body trembled from the terrible effort. The bucket had been squashed like a pancake between his chest and the turbine. His ears were full of water and he wanted to be sick.

The voice of the police chief could be heard in front

of the mill saying, 'Let's go. Portimo will keep guard tonight.'

'He locked his mill, the bastard,' Siponen said, coming back from above the millrace and, with that, the villagers left.

Huttunen stayed sitting in the turbine house until all the voices had died away. Then he slipped outside and disappeared into the forest, the flat oval of his bucket under an arm. He saddled up, hoisting the heavy ruck-sack onto his back, and set off into the forest, wet to the bone. He felt weak and exhausted, but he had to get away from the Suukoski rapids: the search party would already be combing the woods behind the mill.

CHAPTER 20

Huttunen toted his rucksack a couple of miles from the village. He climbed a little hill planted with pines, set up a temporary camp at the top, and made a fire of dead branches to dry his clothes. When he was dressed again, he straightened out the flattened bucket, hammering it into a semblance of shape with a stone the size of a fist, and regretted not having an axe.

It doesn't help not having an axe when you're making a proper camp either. A knife's not much good for chopping fire-wood or dressing poles to make a shelter. In the forest, being without an axe is like having only one arm.

Huttunen put out the fire and hid his rucksack at the foot of a spruce. Constable Portimo had confiscated his axe: well, now he was going to get it back. Huttunen hotfooted it to the village.

As he thought, it wasn't hard slipping into the police

constable's woodshed while its owner was leading the hunt for the fugitive. When the lady of the house went out to do her shopping, leaving the house empty, Huttunen patted the dog and in he went. The impecunious rural police officer's wood store was a pitiful sight. In one corner of the shed was a measly little pile of kindling for the stove that would barely last a day or two. Stacked against the back wall were three steres of damp windfall, which, if they weren't chopped soon, wouldn't have time to dry before winter. And near the door was a vague sprawl of branches, which the police constable had gathered in the woods of neighbouring farmers, not having any land of his own. A sad, flimsy haul.

Portimo's axe was leaning against the wall. It was chipped and rusted, an ugly, unwieldy tool. The crude handle wobbled in its socket, the wedge all dried out and cracked. Huttunen firmed up the wedge, recut the handle and improved the join. Portimo's frame saw was not much better. Huttunen tried it on a log. The blade was blunt and pulled to the right. Oh, the policeman's destitution was painful to behold: an entire woodshed without any dry wood or suitable tools.

It did contain one good bit of equipment, however: an axe he knew very well, his, stuck in the block. The miller took it out, ran his finger along the cutting edge and saw that it was still good and sharp.

Before leaving, Huttunen decided to chop some wood for the police constable as a form of compensation for taking his axe. He ought to help in some way really; after all, the constable was having to run around the woods all day looking for him. He split a big pile of logs, piled them neatly against the wall of the woodshed and, when he saw Portimo's wife coming back from the shop, slipped off into the forest, the gleaming axe over one shoulder.

Huttunen followed the telephone line. The going was easy because there was an old path that used, it seemed, to serve the shop. Keeping to the woods, Huttunen passed Tervola's establishment and carried on under the wires. This was the telephone line the shopkeeper used to set the police on my tail, he thought.

Bloody telegraph poles.

Huttunen gave the offending supports a filthy look. He seemed to hear the shopkeeper's voice in the whirring of the line, his complacent tones putting in an order to his wholesaler in Kemi: meat, sausage, cheese, coffee, tobacco. A wave of blinding hunger overcame Huttunen. He stopped at a pole and resting the blade of his axe against its base, teed up his swing.

'If I cut here, the phone will stop trilling in Tervola's shop.'

The sight of the axe at the base of the pole was so tempting that Huttunen couldn't help striking the quivering wood a blow. All the birds perched on the wire within a radius of a mile flew up into the air. Huttunen swung his axe again, the wires whistled and the whole line reverberated. The heavy pole started to sway and, after a few more blows, cracked at the base and collapsed. The porcelain insulators smashed and, with a noise like a whip crack, the wires flew off into the trees. Huttunen mopped the sweat from his brow and surveyed his handiwork.

The shopkeeper's telephone is now temporarily out of order.

Huttunen tended not to do things by halves. While he was at it, he chopped the pole into eight-foot logs, stacked them on top of each other, rolled up the telephone cable and put it on top of the pile. When the engineers came to repair the line in due course, their job would already be partly done: they'd just have to load the logs onto their cart and put up a new pole.

Now that the shopkeeper's telephone had been silenced, Huttunen decided to take this opportunity to pay him a visit. Tervola would be sure to sell him some supplies this time, especially because, by a happy chance, he had his axe with him.

The shop was pretty full. Its quiet murmur of conversation was replaced by terrorised silence as Huttunen entered, axe in hand. Some customers pretended to be leaving, although most couldn't have had time to buy anything.

Tervola dived into the back of the shop. He could be heard feverishly turning the handle of his telephone and asking for the switchboard. But the connection was cut. No answer from the constable; the police chief couldn't be reached. Tervola came timidly back into the shop.

Huttunen put his axe on the counter and began reeling off the goods he'd come to buy.

'Tobacco, two tins of meat, a pound of salt, sausage, bread.'

The grocer meekly produced the items. As he was weighing the sausage, Huttunen put his axe on the pan of the scales next to the weights, as a joke, and said, 'Look how light this axe is, shopkeeper.'

The axe was such a feature of the miller's shopping trip that the shopkeeper sharply rounded down his bill. As his customer was leaving, Tervola even asked if there was anything else he wanted.

Huttunen turned on the doorstep, 'That will be all, thank you.'

Under cover of the forest, he saw the crowd spill out of the shop. They ran as fast as their legs could take them towards Portimo's house. Huttunen wanted to tuck into the sausage, but it made more sense to get back to camp. Now wasn't the best time for eating.

CHAPTER 21

All day long, dogs' barking and men's shouting echoed through the woods as far as the fugitive's camp. The village had gone on a war footing because of the miller and his escape from the hospital. To get a better view of events, Huttunen climbed a hundred-year-old pine, a venerable colossus towering over the hill where he was hiding. He had to make the climb twice because the first time he forgot his binoculars and couldn't make out what was happening in the village with the naked eye.

Through the lone eyepiece of his binoculars, Huttunen observed intense activity on the village road. Dogs ran around off the lead, men rode in all directions on their bicycles. Farmers stood at crossroads, rifles on their shoulders. There must have been others scouring the forest, but Huttunen couldn't see them from the top of his pine.

The miller climbed down the old tree. As a precaution, he put out the fire and packed his rucksack. The horticulture adviser had promised she would meet him on Leppäsaari Island when it had got dark. But if all that commotion in the village carried on, he thought ruefully, she might not be able to make the rendezvous.

The village did not quieten down until sunset. Then the dogs were tied up and the farmers went home for their suppers and Huttunen set off for Leppäsaari Island.

Someone had been there in the day: the tent had gone. The guy ropes and pegs were scattered between the alders. Huttunen picked up the stakes and wound the rope into a coil.

'People always leave everything lying around.'

Huttunen was afraid Sanelma Käyrämö wouldn't dare come out to the island but she arrived not long after him. The young woman timidly stepped onto the miller's footbridge with a basket over her arm, out of which poked a bottle of milk. Huttunen kissed her and began eating. She filled him in on what had been happening during the day in the village.

Huttunen was now officially a wanted man. He shouldn't have caused a scene in the shop with his axe, she said reproachfully.

'And then you went and weighed the sausage with your axe. Tervola is bound to take you to court for obstructing a commercial transaction. The police chief has had a letter from Oulu saying you've escaped and must be caught. He has told everyone that this is now all extremely official.'

Huttunen finished his meal. But the horticulture adviser had not said all she had to say.

'You chopped down a telegraph pole as well. Engineers have had to be called out from Kemi and the line is still not working. The girl on the switchboard told me that there was a chance you could go to prison for cutting a phone line, if the Post & Telegraph Office was in a bad mood.'

Huttunen remained silent for a long time, staring at the mist on the stream. Then he fetched his wallet from his pocket, took out his savings book and handed it to the adviser.

'I haven't got a bean. Could you go to the bank and take out all the money I've got in my account? It would be too expensive for you to support me in the forest on your wages.'

Huttunen drew up a mandate on a page torn from the blue squared notebook. Sanelma Käyrämö signed under her name and Huttunen added the signature of two witnesses, John Crane and Henry Wolf, both of whom had highly distinctive writing. Huttunen explained that there wasn't a great deal of money in his account, but, if he lived cheaply, he'd have enough to get by until autumn, perhaps even the start of winter.

'I've been thinking of doing more fishing to save money on food.'

She told him not to come back to Leppäsaari Island because their hideaway had been discovered. During the day, Vittavaara had taken Huttunen's tent to the village and given it neatly folded to the police chief. In the evening, the wives of the police chief and the school-teacher had done some washing in the river. Part of their load was Huttunen's mosquito net; the adviser had seen it hanging on the line.

The couple agreed to meet at the Reutu Marsh cross-roads three miles from the church, on the east bank of the Kemijoki. The horticulture adviser promised to cycle there in a week's time. It was a good idea not to see each other for a bit, at least not while the search was in full swing. Especially because the villagers were already keeping an eye on Sanelma Käyrämö.

'Life's not fair . . .' she said. 'The one consolation for me is that your vegetable garden is doing wonderfully. You could pick the carrots today, and the turnips will soon be the size of a person's head. Don't worry, I'll carry on hoeing and manuring your patch. If the village calms down, sweetheart, go and pick some fresh vegetables. They'll provide you with vitamins, my poor Gunnar. You can't imagine how important vitamins are. Especially out here in the forest, they're crucial.'

The horticulture adviser hurried back to the village; Huttunen left Leppäsaari Island and melted into the night.

The following morning, the adviser went to see Huhtamoinen, the manager of the Cooperative Bank. The bank manager asked her to sit down, and almost offered her a cigar, before he thought better of it, quickly shut the box and abstained himself. Sanelma Käyrämö handed him Huttunen's savings book and the mandate.

'The miller Gunnar Huttunen has telephoned me from Oulu and asked me to withdraw all the money from his account. He says he needs it for the hospital canteen.'

Huhtamoinen examined the savings book, smiled with a satisfied air and read the mandate.

'Did Mr Huttunen get these documents to you by telephone as well?'

The adviser replied sharply that the papers had come by that morning's post; the postman Piittisjärvi had brought them.

The bank manager assumed a paternal, almost didactic air.

'As you know, Miss, our work at this bank is governed by the code of confidentiality. I have always made it a point to explain to my staff – that is, to the cashier Sailo and to Miss Kymäläinen – that the banker's code of confidentiality is inviolable. It is a principle more binding than Hippocrates' oath. Generally speaking, to my mind there are three fundamental rules a bank has to abide by. First, a), that is, accounts must be correct down to the last penny. There can be no room for error. Second, b), the bank must have liquid assets. A bank must be financially solid. A lax lending policy does no credit to any establishment, however large it may be. Even where industry is concerned, a bank's support can never be justified if it endangers, however marginally, the financial equilibrium of the bank itself. And third, or c) – this is the main rule – the institution must scrupulously respect bank confidentiality. No information on customers' affairs should leave the bank. Neither without the customer's agreement nor with it. I would say that, in terms of gravity, banker's confidentiality is on a par with military secrecy, especially during peacetime.'

Sanelma Käyrämö didn't understand why Huhtamoinen was giving her a lecture on bank confidentiality. She asked whether the bank manager intended to give her Huttunen's savings or not.

'But everyone knows that the miller Gunnar Huttunen has escaped from Oulu asylum,' Huhtamoinen exclaimed. 'I've got good grounds to think that you, Miss Käyrämö, are in charge of his affairs, now that he is prevented for a variety of reasons from attending to them himself.'

The bank manager locked Huttunen's savings book and mandate away in his safe.

'I must inform you, Miss Käyrämö, that this bank is unable to allow you to withdraw Mr Huttunen's savings. He has been put under guardianship. Furthermore, he is on the run. You will certainly understand that we in the banking profession cannot transfer any funds when the man in question cannot, by virtue of his dementia, come and collect the money in person. In any case, Huttunen has no address. You may know where he is hiding. But I am not asking you where that is; I am not the police. I am a banker and the criminal aspect of this matter does not concern me. No doubt you understand what I am driving at?'

'But it's Huttunen's money,' the adviser tried to argue.

'In theory it does, of course, belong to Huttunen. I do

not deny that. But I will not pay it out to anyone, as I have told you, without official authorisation. In this particular case, the money would quite literally vanish into thin air. What would happen, my dear girl, if all banks were to behave in this manner and transfer their clients' capital and interest to some unknown spot in a marsh or up a hill?'

The horticulture adviser choked back a sob. How was she going to explain this to Huttunen? Huhtamoinen wrote a note on a sheet of paper.

The Cooperative Bank regrets to inform you that it can only pay out your savings and accumulated interest to you in person, and then only on condition the authorities give their express authorisation.

Respectfully yours,

A. Huhtamoinen, Manager

'But, as I've told you, I revere bank confidentiality,' Huhtamoinen continued. 'Should anyone – let's say, for example, Police Chief Jaatila – ask me what brought you here today, I would simply shake my head and remain as silent as the grave. If the police demanded I tell them where Mr Huttunen is hiding, I would keep my counsel, even if I knew where he was. This is how I perceive bank confidentiality, as nothing less than a sacred duty. I would tell the police that you came to ask, ah, for a loan . . . let's say for a sewing machine?'

'I've already got a sewing machine,' sniffed Sanelma Käyrämö.

'Then let's say you came here, ah, to ask my advice
. . . for instance, as to whether it makes sense at present
for an individual to put his or her savings in bonds. And
quite frankly I'd say no, it doesn't. With the situation in
Korea, anyone who has any money would be well advised
to invest it in property. The price of land is soon going
to rise appreciably, unlike the revenue from State bonds.
Everything depends of course on how long the Korean
War lasts, but it doesn't seem as if peace will return to
Asia in the near future, at least not before next summer.
Tell them that's what I said. But now I've moved onto
more general matters, I do beg your pardon, Miss
Käyrämö.'

The horticulture adviser had to leave the bank
manager's office with nothing more than this financial
prognosis to sustain her. She wanted to cry, but swallowed her tears long enough to walk past the bank staff
who were agog with curiosity. It was only when she had
cycled out of the village that Sanelma Käyrämö stopped
her bicycle and burst into endless, despairing sobs. The
bank had taken Gunnar's money and she wouldn't be
paid for at least another two weeks.

CHAPTER 22

Reutu Marsh was a vast expanse of wetland, a giant bog of forming peat that stretched for miles over a maze of shallow, blackwater ponds. A little river, the Sivakka, wound along its western edge at the foot of a modest hill that was known as Mount Reutu.

This was the inviolate spot Huttunen made for, over six miles from the village with more than a league of forest on all sides separating it from the nearest road. He lugged his rucksack to the edge of the marsh, to a gentle bend in the Sivakka where the hill sloped down to the river. The ground was dry and covered in lichen, even though the unstable expanse of bog lay just across the water. It was an ideal place for a camp: beautiful, sheltered and tranquil. A few cranes trumpeted in the distance in the bog. At his back, on the slopes of the hill, pines rustled and, every now and then, trout and grayling could be heard jumping in the languid river.

Huttunen was entranced. He set down his heavy load and, in his mind, christened the spit of land curving out into the river 'Home Point'.

In the days that followed, the miller established a substantial camp on the point. He felled several tall, dead pines, rolling them down the hill to his camp and splitting them into seven-foot logs that he could burn slowly if the nights turned cold and misty.

As shelter, he built a rudimentary hut which he covered with thick fir branches, arranging the butts pointing downwards. He interwove the tips of the branches like scales to form a sturdy roof. From a young birch the diameter of a thigh, he cut a log the length of the hut, and set it down as a windbreak. Abutting this threshold, he laid a soft bed of moss an inch thick, which he spread with small, supple sprigs of fir, stripping out the larger branches so that they wouldn't prick him in the back while he was sleeping.

Huttunen unrolled the saw blade, cut handles for it and strung a length of washing line between them. With his new tool, he sawed off a sturdy pine behind the hut at head height. Using it as a base, he built a store cupboard out of light, dry branches, and left an opening the size of his rucksack on one side. His food, kitchen utensils and rucksack all went into his new larder.

A little way off, at the water's edge, the hermit arranged round rocks the size of a head into a circle. Over this hearth, he made an adjustable frame that automatically kept its position by bending one of the birches on the riverbank. Fifty yards above the camp, at a point where Mount Reutu's slopes grew steeper and one could take in the entire sweep of the marsh, Huttunen nailed a couple of stout planks to two pines, one for a seat and the other for a backrest, and dug a hole almost three foot deep beneath them. This was where, once or twice a day, the hermit's excrement would fall from now on. It became a habit of Huttunen's to stay sitting on the plank longer than he needed, looking at the vast expanse of marsh spread out before him: the cranes striding along in their dignified way; the ducks hurriedly flapping their wings; the groups of five or ten reindeers that would sometimes suddenly come galloping over the banks of earth, fleeing the swarms of mosquitoes in the undergrowth. One day, Huttunen thought he saw a bear at the very edge of the bog. A grey shadow that now and again seemed to rear up on its hind legs. But when he trained his one-eyed binoculars on the horizon, trembling in the summer heat haze, all he saw were cranes. No sign of a bear. Had it left the marsh? Had it ever existed?

Huttunen set up a row of stakes in the long grass on the bank to dry his nets. He cobbled together a precarious raft of dry branches for crossing the river and tethered it, with a pole by the hearth like a sort of pontoon. Finally, the hermit carved a calendar into a dead tree outside the hut. With his axe, he levelled off a rough square of the trunk, one foot wide by two high, planed it smooth and then etched the vertical and horizontal lines of an almanac into the polished surface with a knife. Every morning, he would score the passage of his days into the wood. He did not know the exact date when he finished the camp, but thought it must be near the middle of July. Taking a guess at how much time had passed since Midsummer in the hospital, he chiselled 12, VII into the tree. The blueberries were ripening; that seemed about right.

July was beautiful and hot. The fishing wasn't as good as it had been at the start of spring, or as it would be again in August. The best fish were well fed and mistrustful. The nights were still too bright and the rivers too warm, so the cold-blooded salmonids were drowsy. Huttunen tried his flies, but the trout scorned them. He caught a few pike with spinners, which, if you took the trouble to bake them in the fire, were perfectly fine to eat.

For the fattier fish, Huttunen used nets: he strung them across the river and went downstream to scare the fish into the trap. There were sometimes so many little trout and grayling struggling in the meshes that the hermit would have had plenty left over to salt if he'd had the right container to store them in. He congratulated himself on deciding to bring his plane out here to the back of beyond after all. It would be good to cut and plane some wood for barrel staves in autumn. A few casks of salted fish and all his food problems for the winter would be solved. If it's well salted, trout keeps for more than a season no matter how fatty it is.

Huttunen also thought he'd build a sauna and a little

cabin for winter. He didn't fancy staying cooped up in his hut when the cold set in.

That's a sure-fire recipe for rheumatism.

He pictured the little log cabin, ten foot by ten at the most. A bed and a table would do for furniture, perhaps with a cupboard in the corner and reindeer antlers for coat hooks. In the rear wall, he'd build a corner fireplace out of flat stones, and he'd leave an opening for the window by the door.

I'll have to get a sheet of glass and a few feet of lead piping for the chimney. I don't need asphalted felt; birch bark should last a few years on a cabin roof.

Huttunen went on long hikes from his new camp. He often went up to the top of Mount Reutu with his binoculars to study the village with its little houses and two churches, old and new, big and small. In clear weather, at fixed times on the horizon to the west he could see a plume of smoke rising up into the summer sky from an express. He couldn't hear the engine or see the wagons or the track, but he could tell from the direction of the smoke whether the train was coming from Kemi or Rovaniemi, whether the passengers were heading north or had already seen Lapland.

On the moors around Reutu Marsh, Huttunen picked succulent cranberries from the previous autumn. The yellow brambles in the bog were starting to bud; soon the first berries would appear. It looked as if it would be a bumper crop. There were plenty of ripe blueberries as well. The hermit collected three or four pounds a day in a basket he had plaited out of birch bark. They were delicious in the evening after coffee.

Huttunen made the most of the summer and the peace and quiet. When the weather was fine, sometimes he took his clothes off and sunbathed on top of the hill. He lay down with his trousers folded under his head, and let the sun give him a tan. For hours on end he watched the little clouds passing overhead, constantly changing shape, and saw the most extraordinary animals in them. A mild midday breeze kept the mosquitoes on the other side of the river, in the marsh. Everything was perfectly still. The hermit could almost hear his thoughts colliding in his skull; there were hordes of them, reasonable and unreasonable alike, chasing one another in an endless procession through his mind.

If it rained, Huttunen remained lying in his shelter, listening to heavy raindrops run along the pine needle roof and fall onto the floor. The fire would hiss when they hit the blazing embers, and the hut was lovely and warm. When the rain stopped, the fish would bite. Huttunen didn't even need a net; the trout would hurl themselves at flies right next to the bank.

At night, Huttunen would wake to study the pale, starlit summer sky and start humming. The rumble soon turned into a muffled groaning, and then a savage howl would burst from the hermit's mouth, just like the old days. He felt calmer after it. Howling made him feel less alone. He heard his own voice and it was strange to him, like an animal's.

Sometimes on hot days when he was walking across the endless, treeless expanse of Reutu Marsh, Huttunen would suddenly take to imitating an animal, one of the ones he saw every day, whose behaviour and habits he studied through his binoculars. He would set off at a trot over the sphagnum moss, running in circles with the swaying gait of a male reindeer trying to flee a cloud of insects, and then stop, snorting and grunting and pawing the ground with his hooves. Or else he would spread his wings and furiously take off like a wild goose, gain height, disappear behind the forest and then reappear on the other side of Mount Reutu, another goose now, bracing his webbed feet and coming in to land amid the reeds of a pond, where he'd throw up sheets of muddy water. Or else, becoming a crane, he would stretch his neck, trumpet and, with a keen eye, set about hunting the frogs and shrimps and black-backed pikes that had been washed into the marsh by the spring floods and left captives of the stagnant pools when the waters receded.

When the cranes saw the long-legged man calling in their language in the marsh, they would stop what they were doing, raise their long necks very high and, tilting their heads forward, watch the hermit wandering among their flock, oblivious to the fact that he was imitating a crane for an audience of cranes. The head of the flock sometimes raised its bill to the heavens and let out a long trumpet, a mighty response. Then the hermit would suddenly regain consciousness, become himself again and leave the marsh for his camp. He would smoke a cigarette in his shady hut and think that everything would be fine if his life carried on like this.

If only Sanelma were here.

CHAPTER 23

The week flashed past and suddenly the evening beckoned when the horticulture adviser Sanelma Käyrämö had said she would meet Huttunen at the Reutu Marsh crossroads. In his impatience, the hermit was at the meeting point well before the appointed time. He imagined the young woman's fresh face, her curvaceous figure, her blue eyes and golden hair, her soft, clear voice. He lay down among the trees by the road. Time passed, the mosquitoes bit, but he didn't even notice, such was his sense of expectancy.

About six in the evening, he saw a woman bicycling down the narrow road towards the meeting point. The adviser Sanelma Käyrämö was coming! Huttunen leapt joyfully to his feet and almost ran to meet her, but he restrained himself and didn't go out on the road. They had agreed to meet in the forest, so, keeping his promise, the hermit stayed under the fir trees.

The adviser reached the crossroads. She left her bicycle in the ditch and walked into the forest. Looking nervously around her, she ventured about twenty yards from the road and then stopped uncertainly. Just as Huttunen was about to step forward and take her in his arms, he heard a branch snap in the wood. An elk, a reindeer? No, Vittavaara and Portimo! The two men were stealing furtively through the trees, breathless, their faces bathed in sweat. They crouched down behind a bush without showing themselves to Sanelma Käyrämö. They had clearly been following the adviser all the way from the village through the woods, tracking the hermit and planning to set him a sly trap.

Huttunen moved back and lay down at the foot of a thickly covered fir from where he could see and hear what was happening by the roadside. Although he was trembling with desire, the hermit could not go to Sanelma Käyrämö. The spies were only yards away, wiping the sweat from their foreheads, swatting mosquitoes. It couldn't have been a picnic for them in the woods, trying to keep up with the adviser as she pedalled along a perfectly smooth road.

Did the adviser know she had been followed? Had she stooped to collaborate with the farmers and the police? Was she knowingly the bait? Did she want Huttunen to be sent back to Oulu too, back to that nuthouse sunk in the grimmest apathy and the most morbid inertia?

'Gunnar! Gunnar darling! It's me, I'm here!'

Huttunen did not dare show himself. He hardly dared breathe. He saw Vittavaara was holding a rifle. Did they take him for a murderer? Constable Portimo had sat down on a tree stump to get his breath, but he was keeping a lookout at the same time. Huttunen lay stock-still at the foot of the fir, gritting his teeth. It broke his heart to hear the horticulture adviser calling, 'Gunnar . . . where are you, my poor darling?'

The woman waited for a long time, but as the sombre, silent forest vouchsafed no reply to her persistent appeals, in the end she set down her basket on a tuft of grass, covered it with her scarf and walked sadly back to the road. Vittavaara looked disappointed. He whispered something feverishly to Constable Portimo, which Huttunen could not hear.

With tears in her eyes, the horticulture adviser got back on her bicycle. Huttunen wanted to howl from the depths of his soul, to let out a wilder cry than the biggest wolf, the cruellest pack leader. But he kept silent. The adviser rode off in the direction of the village and soon disappeared round a bend, out of reach.

Since Vittavaara and Portimo hadn't revealed themselves to Sanelma Käyrämö, Huttunen concluded that she wasn't working with them. So, she hadn't betrayed him. Quite the opposite, in fact; she had done just as she had promised the week before and brought him food. Huttunen gazed through bloodshot eyes at the basket of supplies she had left.

As soon as the adviser was out of sight, Vittavaara rushed forward to examine the contents of the hamper. Portimo followed, giving the basket a circumspect glance.

'Shit! Bread and bacon!' Vittavaara exclaimed sourly, tipping the food out onto the grass. Huttunen saw a bottle-of milk and a number of packages wrapped in grease-proof paper. A smell of freshly baked coffee bread wafted into his nostrils.

'And coffee bread too! God almighty!'

Vittavaara ripped open the packages to reveal smoked bacon, saveloy, a packet of coffee and a loaf of bread. At the bottom of the basket were also several pounds of fresh vegetables: turnips, carrots and beetroots. A bunch of marigolds, carefully arranged by Sanelma Käyrämö, rolled onto the ground. Vittavaara grabbed it and waved in the direction of the forest.

'And flowers too, for goodness sake! It's obscene giving flowers to lunatics in the woods!'

Portimo put the provisions back in the basket.

'Listen, Vittavaara . . . the adviser just wanted to make Kunnari happy. Why don't we go? Huttunen isn't going to come now.'

Vittavaara broke a big piece off the lattice of coffee bread and stuffed it in his mouth. After swallowing a few fragrant mouthfuls, he managed to say, 'Taste that! It's unbelievable the delicacies people bring criminals in the woods! Taste it, Portimo!'

Rather than taste it, Portimo wrapped the bun back up in its paper. He put the basket on a tree stump and started to leave. But Vittavaara hooked his arm through the basket handle and, to Portimo's look of disgust, said, 'I don't care if he dies of hunger, I'm not leaving Kunnari this feast.'

To mark his words, he crushed the marigolds he was holding against the trunk of a nearby tree. Portimo looked away – in Huttunen's direction, as chance would have it. The police constable's and hermit's eyes met. Portimo froze, staring fixedly into the forest, then with an awkward cough, looked away and set off for the road from where he called Vittavaara.

With his mouth full, the farmer caught up with Portimo. He put down the basket to sling his rifle over his shoulder, then grabbed the handle and the two of them set off back to the village. Huttunen heard Vittavaara chatting away noisily between mouthfuls of coffee bread. Portimo barely responded, sunk in thoughts of his own.

When Huttunen returned to his camp, weary and ravenous, another inauspicious surprise awaited him. He saw that the raft wasn't in its place by the fire anymore. Someone had taken it to cross the Sivakka and tied it up on the other bank. Who? Why? Remote and secure though it was, had his hideout been discovered? Did the villagers know the whereabouts of his secret camp?

Huttunen forded the rapids upstream, and collected his raft. He found fish remains on the slats: innards and glinting scales. He felt reassured: it must have been just a passing fisherman. The man probably hadn't even noticed the camp through the undergrowth on the bank.

Huttunen moored the raft a hundred yards downstream. Then he went back to his camp and prepared a frugal supper, which he finished off with a bowl of blueberries and a pleasant sprinkling of sugar. But there was nothing pleasant about his thoughts. He was consumed with impotent rage at the farmers of the canton. They had become

169

his persecutors, his hunters, his jailers. If he could only fight them on equal terms, man to man, things would work themselves out. But the law had turned Huttunen into an inferior being, a hermit deprived of all material possessions, even food, to whom love was forbidden. He was hunted like a criminal, the bread was taken out of his mouth; now even the woman he loved was followed like a spy.

Once he had rested, the hermit decided to go and fish at the source of the Sivakka for a day or two. Pike was practically all he caught in the nets by the camp now. He reckoned the waters upstream would be better stocked. He took a supply of reddish flies and a few glittering spinners, some salt and bread as well, figuring he could eat fish all the way up the river, and tucked his axe into his belt.

He left the pretty Home Point with a sense of regret, but while the summer lasted, he had to devote all his time to fishing to prepare for the imminent future, when he would be even more destitute. Setting off along the Sivakka, Huttunen cursed Vittavaara, 'Filthy cake thief.'

CHAPTER 24

The cards had come out at the police chief's. Jaatila had invited Dr Ervinen and the shopkeeper Tervola round for a quiet evening at the games table. They had started with several not particularly exciting board games, but after Dr Ervinen had charged their sherry glasses with a few healthy rounds of his special schnapps, they had decided to continue under the amiable auspices of poker.

The maid, or 'my chambermaid', as Jaatila's wife called her, appeared in the doorway, bobbed in a vague curtsey, and announced that that there was a man to see the police chief. Not wanting to interrupt the game, rather than go into his study the police chief told the maid to show him in. He had three queens, two down on the table, and one still in reserve in his hand. There was one card left to deal. He was already sure of beating the shopkeeper, but Ervinen – Christ almighty, Ervinen might easily have three

171

of a kind. Jaatila raised nonetheless. Ervinen blanched. But he could just have been pretending to be unnerved. Damn you, you old crook, thought the police chief.

It was at this juncture that a man reeking of smoke and fish guts entered the room. The police chief asked him what he wanted at this time of the night. The man explained that he had been fishing by Mount Reutu, on public land, of course.

'Was it good, the fishing?' the police chief asked distract-edly, drawing his last card. It was a six of diamonds, not the missing queen, but there was no point letting his opponents know that. His was still the best hand on the table, with two queens showing. The shopkeeper folded, but Ervinen, who looked as if he was working up a straight flush, saw him and raised him again. He pushed the price of a nice rifle into the kitty.

'The fishing was good, yes,' said the man in the doorway, craning his neck to follow the game. He could see Ervinen's cards over his shoulder but nothing in his face showed what sort of hand the doctor might have. The police chief looked him in the eye and raised his eyebrows, but the fellow just looked away.

'So, the fishing was good, was it?' said the police chief, seeing Ervinen. The cards went down on the table; Ervinen had been bluffing. His first card was a paltry two of spades. The police chief scooped the pot: that was the cold, hard truth of the matter. He poured everyone a drink, apart from the visiting fisherman, who he asked in an official tone, 'So what brings you here?'

The man said that he had found a brand new raft on the banks of the Sivakka.

'Who could have made that, I asked myself? And when I nosed around, guess what I found? An entire camp, also just made. That's what I've come to tell you, Chief of Police, there's a wild man living by the river.'

The police chief couldn't see what concern some camp in the woods was of his.

'The forest is full of rafts and huts. I'm hanged if that's got anything to do with the police.'

Taken aback, the fishermen retreated to the door, from where he said apologetically, 'I just thought that it might be Gunnar Huttunen, the crazy miller, who'd made the camp. Because I heard in the village that he'd escaped from the asylum and that he was hiding in the woods.'

Ervinen's ears pricked up immediately and he called the man back. He asked him what the camp looked like.

'It was brand new and looked well made. There was a hut with a simple pitched roof. And a woodpile with enough wood for a few weeks. And then there was a little stillroom on a tree trunk. I even found a shithole in the woods, and the raft by the bank, as I told you at the start.'

'What sort of workmanship was it, the raft and all the rest?' asked the police chief.

'It looked like a carpenter had done it. Even the seat for the privy was planed off properly. There were stakes on the bank to dry a couple of nets as well.'

'It's Huttunen,' Ervinen said. 'The miller is good with

his hands, even if the rest of his motor skills are completely haywire. Let's go and catch him in his hideout.'

The police chief telephoned Constable Portimo, telling him to collect a few men and meet him at his office. Armed. They'd go in two cars.

Half an hour later, a group of men stood outside the police station: Portimo, Siponen, Vittavaara, the schoolteacher Tanhumäki – even the farmhand Launola had been enlisted. Siponen, Vittavaara and Launola got into the doctor's car; the others went with the police chief. They took the informer, stinking of fish, as a guide. The men drove at high speed to the Reutu Marsh crossroads, where they got out of the car. Night had fallen, but it wasn't yet too dark.

The police chief briefly gave his orders. They were going to take Huttunen by surprise. They would surround the camp, destroy it and take its occupant prisoner. The fisherman would show them the way. They must observe complete silence to ensure their quarry didn't take fright and make a run for it.

'Can we shoot if he runs off into the woods?' Siponen asked the police chief, flourishing his punt gun.

'We're going to try and surprise him, but if he attacks, you can shoot. That's a case of legitimate self-defence. At the legs first, though, and only the stomach or head after that.'

The search party reached the Sivakka just before midnight. The men fanned out into a loose line and squelched upriver towards the place where the informer said he'd found the camp. They soon reached the raft. The guide reported that it had been moved downstream.

In a low voice, the police chief ordered some of the men to work their way round the camp, while the others stayed put. The riverbank was left unguarded, they thought that even Huttunen wasn't mad enough to throw himself into a stream bordering that sort of bog. The siege party silently surrounded the camp; at the police chief's signal, a hazel grouse call, they began to move in. They crawled over the damp ground on their hands and knees, getting soaked in the process, but they were so excited no one thought of complaining.

In half an hour the camp was encircled. The police chief gave the signal to charge. Yelling and thundering, nine armed men burst out of the dark forest.

But the camp was deserted. No one was asleep in the hut. The trap had snapped shut on thin air . . . The storm troops crowded round the fisherman to give their respective opinions of the reliability of his tip-off. The man said he was going home and disappeared into the woods.

Vittavaara took the rucksack out of the storeroom and emptied its contents onto the ground. He examined each object meticulously, as if it would reveal whether it belonged to Huttunen. Portimo glanced at the rucksack and tersely declared it was Kunnari's.

'He had the same rucksack when we went capercaillie shooting at Puukko Hill last winter, two Sundays in a row. We got half a dozen each time, and we didn't have a dog between us. Amazing, eh?'

'As a representative of law and order, you've got pretty poor taste in your hunting friends,' the police chief muttered.

'Kunnari hadn't escaped from the hospital back then,' Portimo protested.

The police chief ordered the men to mount guard over the camp. They retreated into the wood, where they were told not to smoke or speak but to lie in the dark undergrowth without making a noise and wait for Huttunen to return to the camp. Everyone thought he would only be gone for a while, and that, if they kept a lookout, they'd easily catch him by surprise.

But the men remained in the thicket without moving a muscle all night, and still no sign of Huttunen. Stiff with cold and damp, they gathered in the early morning in the middle of the camp for a conference.

'It's pointless keeping watch any longer,' Ervinen burst out, infuriated. 'He's smelled the trap ... Perhaps he's watching us now from behind a tree, and having a good laugh at our expense. Anyway, as far as I'm concerned, I'm not lying in a soaking bog because of a madman any longer.'

Launola eagerly agreed with the doctor, prompting Siponen to snap at his hired man, 'You'll lie in wait for Huttunen until Christmas if I tell you to. I am the one who you pays you, you good-for-nothing.'

'Just because I happen to work for you doesn't mean I have to do any old thing. This isn't a bit like haymaking or tree-felling; this is like being at the front.'

The police chief put a stop to the argument by declaring that there seemed to be no sense continuing the surveillance. The hermit had got wind of something and was hiding; they should destroy the camp, that was all they could do. The men set to work with a will.

Vittavaara shouldered Huttunen's rucksack. Siponen pulled down the hut and chucked the branches into the river. Ervinen and the schoolteacher dismantled the larder, which was also consigned to the Sivakka. Launola's responsibility was the seat on the hillside; he took it upon himself to fill in the cesspit as well, after the police chief had counted Huttunen's faeces and worked out from them how long the camp had been occupied. On the riverbank, the hearthstones were rolled into the water, the frame cut and the stakes for drying the nets snapped. As a final touch, they unmoored Huttunen's raft, which was duly carried off by the current. The one thing they didn't wreck was the calendar the hermit had carved into the trunk of the dead tree. By comparing it with his diary, the police chief established that the last mark had been made two days earlier.

'Now he's lost all his gear, Huttunen will have to show himself in the village,' Police Chief Jaatila said. 'I'd advise everyone here to be on the alert over the coming days. For the safety of the village, we have to arrest this dangerous lunatic as quickly as possible and get him proper medical care.'

Their work of destruction complete, the men set off home just as Huttunen was approaching his camp. He was walking along the riverbank, carrying over twenty pounds of fish on a stick. He was in excellent spirits, and thought the first thing he'd do when he got to Home Point was to make himself a nice cup of coffee.

CHAPTER 25

The devastation of Home Point was a bitter blow. Everything the hermit had put up had been systematically torn apart. All his belongings had been taken; nothing had been spared. Huttunen went over every inch of his former camp without finding anything he could use. His raft had been pushed out into the current; even his privy's wooden seat had been sawed through and the hole beneath stopped up.

Terrible curses fell from Huttunen's lips.

Once again his life was at a total impasse. He knew it would be impossible to hide in the forest for long without the right gear or any protection against the rigours of the wild. All he had were the clothes he stood up in, a few flies and spinners, a knife and an axe.

The hermit guessed that the police chief and the local farmers had discovered his camp and levelled it. Gripping the handle of his axe until his knuckles turned white, he fixed the gleaming blade with a murderous stare.

Huttunen grilled some fish on a stick over a fire. It was paltry fare, especially since they'd taken the salt in the rucksack. He washed it down with river water.

Afterwards he buried the remains of the fish in the embers of the fire and abandoned Home Point. He spent the following night at the top of Mount Reutu, sleeping on a carpet of pine needles. Woken by the cold in the early hours of the morning, he climbed onto the highest rock on the hill and looked furiously towards the village.

The little place was sleeping peacefully. The men who had destroyed the hermit's camp were snug in their warm beds. Huttunen set up a menacing howl, muffled at first, and then at the top of his voice, a thunderous, demented bellow. Carrying in the clear summer night, the crazed wail reached the village. The dogs woke up and started barking, their manes bristling. Soon all of them were giving voice, even the smallest runt, yapping and barking with all their might in reply to Huttunen's howling as it rang out, clear as day, from the rocks of Mount Reutu. In the distance the barking could be heard spreading from place to place and the dogs for miles around did not quieten down until the early morning, by which time Huttunen himself had gone back to sleep on the pine needles of Mount Reutu.

No one slept that night in the village. Farmers went out in their socks onto their front porches to listen to the howling, and then came back and said to their wives, 'That's Kunnari howling out there.'

The wives sighed anxiously and said, 'You should have left him in peace. He's complaining because all his belongings have been stolen, poor soul.'

In the morning, Police Chief Jaatila telephoned the Siponens and requested Sanelma Käyrämö come to his office; he had some questions he wanted to ask her.

But the police chief couldn't get anything conclusive out of Käyrämö. The horticulture adviser didn't know where Gunnar Huttunen could be at that moment. Jaatila officially cautioned her that it was against the law to help the hermit. Huttunen needed medical care and order had to be restored in the village. Throughout the interview, the police chief yawned and drank strong coffee. With all the racket Huttunen and the village dogs had made last night, he hadn't been able to sleep a wink either.

Later that day, Police Chief Jaatila and Constable Portimo went with dogs to Mount Reutu to track Huttunen. But the mutts didn't seem to realise they were meant to follow the hermit's trail. Despite being given his clothes to smell, they hared off up the hill after a squirrel. In a fit of pique, Police Chief Jaatila blazed away at the animal with his pistol, although a rodent's pelt is hardly a prize. Small game is not easy to hit with a handgun. The police chief fired a full round at the bundle of red fur fleeing from tree to tree with the dogs at its heels. Mount Reutu echoed with gunfire as he furiously stalked the bushy-tailed runaway, but to no avail. His prey escaped when he ran out of ammunition, and it was eventually Constable Portimo, to the dogs' rapturous delight, who picked off the squirrel with his rifle. He handed the bloody little corpse to the police chief, but his superior spurned the gift and chucked the creature savagely into the bushes.

The dogs then refused to leave the woods, so the police chief left Portimo on Mount Reutu with the job of rounding up the rampaging pack. On his way back to the village, he had to explain to everyone he met what all the shooting had been about. He was in a foul temper by the time he shut himself away in his office.

Appropriately enough, the telephone rang just at that moment. It was Oulu mental hospital asking if the police had found one of their neurasthenic patients, a certain Huttunen. Jaatila grunted into the receiver that the man had not been caught yet, although it was not for want of trying.

'Why in hell's name did you let that lunatic escape? You're supposed to have solid brick walls and locks on the doors in your place, and yet you let people walk out just as they please. You'd do better to keep a closer eye on your inmates!'

The hospital official retorted coldly that the mental patient was not from Oulu, he was a resident of the police chief's canton, a place where it appeared madmen occupied positions other than just that of miller, and consequently it was the police chief's job to detain him. Acid and fruitless comments were then exchanged at length on the subject of who was responsible for Huttunen's capture until the police chief finally slammed down the receiver in exasperation.

Huttunen did not howl the following night, but instead went to the village. He stole through the houses to the Suukoski rapids where he picked a few root vegetables – turnips and carrots – from his garden to stave off his hunger. He didn't go into the mill because he was afraid it was guarded.

The Siponens' foul-tempered spitz did not wake up when Huttunen sneaked round to the back of the farm through the forest. Everyone was asleep on the ground floor, but there was a light shining on the floor above. The horticulture adviser was still awake then. Huttunen threw a pebble at the window and ducked into some currant bushes to wait. The light soon went out. The window opened and the adviser's curly hair appeared. She peered out into the garden, her eyes swollen from crying. Huttunen came out of the bushes and softly called up to his beloved, 'Did you get my money out of the bank, Sanelma darling? Throw it down to me!'

The young woman shook her head sadly and whispered a reply. Then, seeing that Huttunen couldn't hear, she dropped a small piece of paper down into the garden. Huttunen grabbed it, and saw written:

The Cooperative Bank regrets to inform you that it can only pay out your savings and accumulated interest to you in person.

Respectfully yours,
A. Huhtamoinen, Manager

* * *

Huttunen couldn't understand a word of it. Gesticulating indignantly, he fired off questions in a furious whisper until the Siponens' dog woke up with a start by the front door and began barking in a sleepy voice. Sanelma Käyrämö took fright, scribbled a few words on a scrap of paper and threw it down to Huttunen. He read:

Dear Gunnar,
Meet me tomorrow evening at six in the forest, behind
Vittavaara's milk shed.

The hermit retreated into the forest to consider the situation. The dog's barking had woken Siponen. In his underpants, rifle in hand, he came out into the garden, checked the woodshed and sauna, looked at the forest where the dog was staring and then, when the hound had stopped barking, scolded the creature and went back into the house in his stockinged feet.

Huttunen ate a few turnips, cutting thin slices with his knife. He tried to understand why on earth the bank manager had refused to give his money to the adviser. What gave Huhtamoinen the right to act so maliciously? Huttunen was seized with fury at the man. He hid the rest of the turnips in a hole in the moss and ran off through the woods to the bank.

The Cooperative Bank occupied the ground floor of a stone building. The manager lived on the first floor with his wife and children, and probably one of his employees as well: it seemed far too big for just one family. Huttunen studied the building housing his worldly fortune, and wondered how he could get in and retrieve his property. Clearly the only key to that safe was a few sticks of dynamite. The sensible course of action, therefore, would be to settle his business during opening hours. But there was no point going there empty-handed. A plain old axe seemed too far too humdrum a weapon for the situation. A rifle would be a more reliable guarantee at the counter to get what he was owed.

Huttunen remembered Ervinen's magnificent gun collection. He could easily pinch one from it. The doctor would still have plenty for his own purposes, especially since the hunting season hadn't yet started.

The following evening, Huttunen met the horticulture adviser in the woods behind Vittavaara's milk shed. She was so scared she was trembling. Huttunen whispered lovingly in her ear, put a protective arm round her shoulders, reassured her and asked her how she was bearing up. Sanelma Käyrämö recounted all the terrible things that had happened since their last meeting. She tried to give Huttunen money but he refused.

'You get paid such a pittance, my poor sweetheart, you keep it. I'll work out a way to get some myself.'

Huttunen asked the adviser to ring Dr Ervinen that evening and tell him he was urgently needed fifteen miles away at Lake Kanto.

'Tell him a doctor's needed for a forceps birth at Puukko Hill farm, for the maid.'

When the adviser asked why she had to tell the doctor

such a pack of lies, Huttunen explained that he wanted Ervinen to be out of his house for a while. If he were called out to somewhere remote, Huttunen would have enough time to explore the doctor's surgery.

'I need some of Ervinen's pills. He's got some sedatives in the cabinet near the fireplace. I saw him take them out of there last time.'

Sanelma Käyrämö could see that Huttunen might need a tranquilliser. But that didn't make her the less afraid.

'It's still stealing . . . and it's not right to make anonymous calls to the doctor. Anyway, no one's expecting a child at Kanto Lake, they haven't even got a girl working on the farm.'

Huttunen convinced the young woman to do as he asked. Wasn't it, indirectly, a form of medical care? He was ill, after all; no one could deny that. Obviously it wasn't entirely legal, but the end justified the means. His head wouldn't be able to take the pressure much longer. And if he went to the chemist to buy medicine, they'd throw him in a cell straightaway and send him back to the asylum by the first train, wouldn't they?

Sanelma Käyrämö promised to call Ervinen that evening. She was afraid the doctor would recognise her, but Huttunen assured her that all women could disguise their voices, since even most men could do at least a couple of different accents.

'OK, I'll call. I wouldn't dare say Puukko Hill farm, but there is a Leena Lankinen at Kanto Lake who is pregnant. I'll say it looks as if she might miscarry.'

186

The horticulture adviser described her visit to the bank and said that the police chief had interrogated her and harried her with questions and threats. Huttunen was furious; this was an abuse of power too far.

'Why do they have to take it out on an innocent woman? You haven't escaped from a mental hospital. You're perfectly sane. Can't they at least leave women in peace? Isn't it enough hounding me day and night?'

As the couple parted, the adviser gave Huttunen a kiss and half a pound of smoked bacon. Huttunen remained in the forest in transports of happiness, the delicious piece of bacon in his hand and the memory of the adviser's warm kiss on his lips. After Sanelma Käyrämö had ridden off on her bicycle, the hermit took the meat out of its greaseproof paper and ate it all, including the rind, such was his hunger.

CHAPTER 26

Huttunen's pocket watch showed eight o'clock. The hermit was lying in wait in the woods behind Ervinen's house, from out of which the doctor should rush out at any moment, urgently required for a possible miscarriage at Kanto Lake.

Sure enough, just after eight the doctor left the house, looking hurried and annoyed. He was carrying his doctor's bag and wearing gumboots. The horticulture adviser Sanelma Käyrämö had raised the alarm then. Ervinen cranked up the starter handle of his car and sped off towards Kanto Lake. As soon as he was out of sight, Huttunen tried the front door of the house. It was locked so he had to climb in through the cellar window.

Once inside, he went straight to the back room to choose a good hunting gun. He was spoilt for choice: hanging on the wall were a shotgun, a precision rifle, a rifle for shooting elk, a hunting rifle and a combination gun, one barrel for cartridges and the other for bullets. Huttunen decided to take just one, the hunting rifle. He found plenty of ammunition in the desk drawer. A light rifle was perfect. He could shoot an elk with it if he had to, but it wasn't too powerful for game birds either.

Huttunen decided to take some other things while he was at it. He would compensate the doctor for his loss one day, he thought, but for the moment, needs must, because he couldn't survive in the forest without the right equipment. Well, here it all was, and who was going to stop him? The police chief and the villagers – with Ervinen leading the way – had taken everything he owned. He was just paying them back.

Ervinen had a superb rucksack, far superior to the one seized from Huttunen. It made sense, he supposed, that a doctor would have a better rucksack than a simple miller. His fishing tackle also passed muster. There could have been more flies, but the collection of spinners was fantastic. There was so much camping equipment that it was hard to choose. Huttunen crammed it all in, and then went into the bedroom and got a thick blanket, which he rolled up and tied on top of the rucksack. He took a pair of new, high-magnification binoculars that were hanging on the wall. A compass and map bag containing topographical surveys of the area added to the hermit's haul.

When he'd packed everything he needed, Huttunen had a last look around, as one does before leaving one's home to make sure one hasn't forgotten anything. He thought it might be polite to leave a note on the table, explaining what had happened in the house and why. But then he remembered the systematic destruction of his camp and furiously dismissed the idea.

No one left a note of apology at Reutu Marsh. Now it's this quack's turn to suffer! Why did he have to go and certify me in the first place anyway?

Huttunen left the house the way he had come in. He passed silently from the garden to the forest and, skirting the village, headed towards the banks of the Kemijoki. It would be sensible to spend the night west of the river: they'd be looking for him out in the isolated country around Mount Reutu.

His days of taking the public ferry across the Kemijoki being over, the hermit had to borrow a boat moored by the bank, which he rowed to the other side and hid under some trees at the mouth of a stream. A mile or so from the river, he found a dense fir forest where he spent the night wrapped in Dr Ervinen's blanket. In the morning, he went back to the boat, this time only taking the rifle and a couple of handfuls of cartridges. He pushed the craft into the water.

Time to go to the bank.

The hermit slipped through the woods like a ghost to the rear of the village bank. It was so early the branch wasn't even open. Huttunen decided to wait for office hours and loaded his rifle.

As soon as the bank opened, he went in holding the gun. The staff panicked: the cashier flew like an arrow into the backroom, calling Huhtamoinen the bank manager, and leaving one deathly pale teller at the counter convinced he was about to die. A mentally ill person entering the bank with a gun in his hand seemed justifiable cause for alarm. But rather than riddling the place with bullets, Huttunen calmly informed the clerk, 'I have come to withdraw my savings. The full amount, including interest.'

The bank manager Huhtamoinen rushed to the front of the counter. Beside himself with anxiety, he protested, 'Mr Huttunen, you, here . . . The money in your account is on the premises, of course, in our safe, but I shouldn't pay it out to you, in fact . . .'

Huttunen made as if to cock his rifle.

'That money's mine. I don't want anybody else's. I'll just take what I'm owed.'

Terrified, Huhtamoinen stammered, 'I don't in the slightest dispute that you have a savings account with us and that there's money in it too . . . but . . . but it's been sequestrated. The commune's guardianship board has transferred it to its own account. We received notice from Oulu that you had been put under guardianship . . . You have to obtain the farmer Vittavaara's consent to withdraw your money. Why don't I telephone him? Perhaps he'll authorise the payment.'

'No one's ringing anyone. You'd just ring the police chief anyway. And what the hell has Vittavaara got to do with my money, in any case? Isn't the revenue from his forest enough for him?'

The bank manager explained that Vittavaara was the president of the commune's guardianship board and hence took the decisions concerning the financial affairs of the people under its guardianship.

'Other than that, all this fuss over accounts leaves me completely cold,' swore Huhtamoinen.

'I'm still taking my money,' Huttunen said. 'Where do I sign?'

With a trembling hand, the teller slid a receipt over the counter. Huttunen signed and dated it. Huhtamoinen counted the money out on the table. It wasn't much, but it would do for a few months.

The cashier's voice could be heard in the back room. Huttunen went to see what he was doing and found him talking on the telephone. This wasn't the ideal time to make a call, Huttunen pointed out. The terrified employee hung up.

Having sorted out his financial affairs, the hermit told Huhtamoinen that if he had any spare money in the future, he'd put it in Government bonds rather than give it to a bank.

'I don't trust institutions that only allow you access to your savings if you've got a gun.'

Huhtamoinen sought to play down the incident.

'On no account can the bank be considered at fault here. We are merely obliged to observe the law and follow the authorities' instructions, however harsh and disagreeable an obligation that may be ... This whole business has mainly been a question of misunderstandings. But you mustn't lose your trust in us, Mr Huttunen. I wouldn't even go so far as to call this intervention of your's armed robbery, it's really something quite different. When this matter is cleared up, I hope you'll come back and conduct your finances through our bank. We think of all our old clients as friends, I can assure you. I feel we could even discuss the possibilities of a loan . . . in the future, of course.'

Huttunen slipped back into the forest.

Everyone in the bank was frozen in shock for a moment, and then the cashier ran to telephone the police chief. The bank manager reported the crime in person. Gunnar Huttunen had just forced his way into the bank, armed with a rifle, he said.

'He robbed the bank. He didn't get away with a big haul – his savings should cover it without difficulty – but holding up a bank is a serious crime, and I trust you will mount a search party and go after him. Huttunen has only just vanished into the woods.'

CHAPTER 27

The hermit ran through the woods behind the village to the banks of the Kemijoki. He jumped into the boat and, oars flying, launched out into the turbulent river. The police chief was bound to organise a huge manhunt; he had no time to lose.

The news of Huttunen's visit to the bank had already crossed the river, as the line of cars queuing for the ferry testified. A dozen or so men were already on board with their bicycles and most of them had a gun over their shoulders. Huttunen came level with the ferry two hundred-odd yards downstream.

'Hey there, mate!' the passengers shouted at him. 'Come to the village with us. Kunnari Huttunen has robbed the bank and stolen Ervinen's fishing tackle and rifle!'

When Huttunen continued pulling hard on the oars

without replying, someone said, 'He can't hear. Shout louder.'

The passengers bellowed so loud that Huttunen was forced to stop rowing and give them an answer. He pulled his cap over his eyes and yelled, 'I'm off to the station, then I'll be with you!'

This was enough for the men; Huttunen was able to make his getaway. He pulled the boat up onto the banks of the stream and raced into the woods. Time was short. It was lucky no one from the ferry had recognised him. The hermit collected his rucksack, studied Ervinen's maps for a moment and then plunged into the tall trees west of the Kemijoki in the direction of Puukko Hill. Surrounded on three sides by vast expanses of marshland, with a little stream at the foot of one of its slopes, Puukko Hill was a good eight miles away. Huttunen thought he'd be safe there, at least at first. The police chief would have to recruit hundreds of men if he wanted to comb all the forest between the village and Puukko Hill. Beside, he'd look east of the Kemijoki first, in the wilds of Reutu Marsh.

Huttunen spent the day lazing on Puukko Hill. As its name – Knife Hill – suggested, it was a tall hill covered with slender firs, their crowns tapered like sharpened blades. From time to time, Huttunen trained his binoculars east, past Puukko Brook and the great marshes, to see if his pursuers had picked up his trail.

Huttunen counted and re-counted his money. To the last penny, it was the exact amount he had saved over the years, plus interest. The hermit thought he'd buy a few things in the neighbouring canton when the forest calmed down. Ervinen's fishing gear would do for the moment, and, all things being well, he should be able to bag a few birds for the pot. He examined the gun. What a beautiful rifle: high quality workmanship, with a five-bullet magazine and a telescopic sight. But now wasn't the moment to try it; any shooting would put the trackers in the forest on his tail.

Towards evening, Huttunen started: his binoculars had caught a glimpse of someone moving. A hunched little man had suddenly popped up on the other side of the peat bog with what appeared to be a heavy load on his back. Huttunen focused on the figure. What was he carrying? The man seemed to be bowed under the weight of a huge container, a sort of black barrel. It was at least a mile from the edge of the marsh to the hill, so it was difficult to be sure. But the man was evidently in a terrible hurry. He was running along, sinking into the shifting bog at every step, barely stopping to take a breath despite his burden. He was heading straight across the marsh to Puukko Hill. Huttunen loaded his rifle and waited. If the man was alone, as he seemed to be, there was no need to make a run for it immediately. Nonetheless he still hid his rucksack among some rocks on the banks of Puukko Brook.

The man drew nearer, half running. Huttunen saw through his binoculars that he was carrying a pitch-black drum, with a capacity of at least ten gallons. A muffled metallic clinking echoed up from the marsh in time with his steps. The man seemed to have some sort of poles or pipes under his arm. Eventually the fellow stopped within firing range of the hill, set down his load, took a few deep breaths and then ran back in the direction he had come from. With nothing to carry, he fairly shot along. Oh, he was in a hell of a rush, this little chap.

Huttunen was amazed: why had he dragged this barrel all the way out here, to the middle of this desolate marsh? Why was he working himself into such a lather?

The oddball disappeared into the woods on the other side of the marsh. Huttunen wanted to have a look at what he'd been carrying, but something stopped him. Who knew why that equipment had been dragged there so laboriously? Perhaps it was a giant bomb designed to arouse his curiosity, the hermit thought, a trap.

Man's cruelty and cunning knows no bounds: I'd better keep a safe distance from that paraphernalia as long as I can.

After a while, the man emerged from the woods by the marsh with another load, possibly even heavier than the first one, on his back. So that's why he went off – more supplies to ferry across this bog. Huttunen studied the man's bizarre behaviour through his binoculars. This time he was carrying a gleaming container. It was smaller than the previous one, and so heavy that he hadn't the strength to run, but he was walking fast, straight towards Puukko Hill and the black barrel awaiting him on the moss.

When the man came closer, Huttunen saw that he was toting a five-gallon milk churn. It looked full, judging by how far his feet sunk into the marsh. He dropped it on the ground when he reached his first load, caught his breath, and then hoisted the black barrel onto his back. Huttunen swapped his binoculars for his rifle, released the safety catch and waited to see what would happen next. The man seemed to be making a beeline for Huttunen's lookout point. The miller took cover in the spruces, ready to fire. How could he tell what the mysterious churn carrier's intentions might be?

It was only when the fellow climbed the hill that Huttunen recognised him. The tub hauler was none other than the village postman Piittisjärvi! Huttunen knew him well, as did everyone in the village. He was a good man, albeit a hopeless drunk – although how many men, good and bad alike, haven't taken that path and been lost to drink? Huttunen relaxed: the newcomer with all his baggage had definitely not been sent by Police Chief Jaatila. Piittisjärvi was a skinny little guy in his fifties who had been widowed before the war; a jolly sort, not up to much, who lived on his meagre postman's salary and was always short of money but rarely of strong drink. He often staggered when he delivered letters, and dropped off packages with a pitiful hangover. When he was sober, he was a quiet, rather obliging soul, but if he'd been drinking, many a local dignitary was the recipient of a few choice home truths from their postman, since alcohol spurred Piittisjärvi to put into words what he thought of those who life had treated more kindly than him.

Panting heavily, Piittisjärvi climbed the hill. He set the sooty barrel and some pipes down on the moss. Steam rose off him like an exhausted horse; his hands trembled from the intensity of the exertion. His features were drawn; sweat rolled down his wrinkles. He wiped his face with his filthy sleeve and stood with his hand pressed to his chest for a moment. A thick cloud of mosquitoes had followed him from the marsh but he was too tired to shoo the bloodsuckers away. Then he span on his heel and set off back to the marsh to get the churn he'd left there.

When Piittisjärvi had managed to drag every last bit of kit and caboodle onto the hill, he finally calmed down, sat on the lid of the churn and took out a cigarette. He was so shattered that he couldn't light it until the third go, his trembling fingers snuffing out the first two matches.

'Oh shit!'

The man was exhausted and in a foul temper, which did not much surprise Huttunen. Dragging a load like that God knows how far over an unstable bog would cast a shadow over the most genial of spirits. The hermit stepped out from the trees holding his rifle.

'Hey, Piittisjärvi.'

The postman was so afraid that his cigarette tumbled onto the moss. But when he recognised Huttunen, his fears evaporated and an exhausted smile lit up the fellow's lined face.

'Kunnari, my God! So this is where you've got to.'

Piittisjärvi retrieved his cigarette and offered Huttunen one. The hermit asked the postman what he was doing on Puukko Hill. And what the devil were those tubs he was dragging around way out here in the woods?

'Haven't you ever seen a still?'

Piittisjärvi explained that he'd set up his secret distillery in its usual place on Mount Reutu. The mash had already fermented, and he had decided he was going to boil it that very morning. Until, that is, the peace of the forest was shattered at crack of dawn: men were scouring the hillside with rifles on their shoulders; dogs were barking; shouts of Huttunen's name and rallying shots ringing out in all directions. The whole place had been in uproar.

'You can imagine, I got out of there double quick. I had to evacuate the whole works. I've been dragging it through the woods ever since, east of the Kemijoki first, then I took it over the river in a boat, but that nearly sunk in the chaos, then all the way here, going like the clappers all day! I tell you, you won't get a minute's peace in the woods east of the river now. I've never been in such hot water in all my life.'

Piittisjärvi took a long drag on his cigarette. He looked at his churn of fermented mash, his vat and his tubes and smiled blissfully.

'But I snatched my still from their clutches, those curs. During the war, I found myself in a bit of a similar predicament during the retreat. Me and another guy had stayed behind on the isthmus with a machine gun. When we finally scarpered, it was a hell of a job dragging that thing. But lugging my set-up this time was harder. That's twice now I've had to run all day to escape from fellows with guns.'

Huttunen was moved by Piittisjärvi's plight. He'd never meant to put the postman to so much trouble, he said, but the amiable fellow cut him short with a benevolent wave.

'Don't worry, Kunnari. I'm not blaming you, the rural police chief is the real cause of all this carry-on. Here you go, have another cigarette!'

CHAPTER 28

That night, Piittisjärvi and Huttunen set up the postman's still in the bushes on the banks of the Puukko. Piittisjärvi was all for putting the mash on to boil straightaway; it had fermented and his mouth was terribly dry. But the night was clear and windless; any smoke rising up from the banks of the stream could give away the site of the distillery. It was not until morning, after a wind had picked up, therefore, that they lit a little wood fire under the vat and poured in the strong-smelling brew. Huttunen used the empty churn to fetch water from the stream and fill the cooling tub. As soon as the alcohol vapour reached the tubes, it condensed and began to flow, drop by drop, into the waiting container.

Piittisjärvi tasted the first distillate, grimaced with delight and handed the mug to Huttunen. But the hermit declined, explaining that at that moment sobriety struck him as a good thing.

'You're mad not to want any of this nectar,' the drunkard exclaimed in amazement. But after briefly mulling over the pros and cons of his partner's abstinence, he made no further attempts to change his mind.

'More for me this way.'

Huttunen decided to cast a few flies in the stream. Before going, he took another churn of cold water to the still.

On his return with two salmon trout, Huttunen found Piittisjärvi entering an already advanced state of intoxication. The postman suggested that, as the more lucid of the two of them, the hermit should take charge of the cooking while he devoted his time to getting conscientiously hammered.

Before the postman could fulfil his part of the bargain, however, Huttunen grilled the fish on the fire under the still. Piittisjärvi had some salt and bread, as well as a piece of salted bacon. They ate the trout's pink flesh in their fingers, sprinkling salt on its sizzling skin, and accompanying it with mouthfuls of bread. Huttunen realised that he hadn't had a decent meal in a long time; not since his camp in Reutu Marsh had been destroyed. As for Piittisjärvi, he had last eaten two days previously, when he had gone to the post office to pick up the letters and newspapers. But he didn't tend to eat much in summer in general, anyway, what with all the mail he had to deliver and alcohol he had to distil.

'I eat better in winter, when I'm not so busy. I cook almost every day when it's cold, even though it's just me.'

Piittisjärvi proposed a collaboration of mutual benefit, whereby Huttunen would supervise the still while he did his job as a postman. Piittisjärvi had to deliver the mail to the station and two neighbouring villages three days a week, which left him barely enough days to brew his moonshine, given that he also needed time to drink it. In return for Huttunen working the still, therefore, he would see to every aspect of the hermit's mail. Huttunen asked what sort of mail he could expect in this forlorn place.

'Just take out a subscription to the *Northern News*! We'll put your letterbox in the woods by the station. I'll deliver you your newspapers and letters just like anyone else. And you can send letters too; I'll see they get there. Why don't you write to the new horticulture adviser? Apparently she's taken a real shine to you.'

Huttunen thought it over. He should write to Sanelma; it wasn't a bad idea. As for newspapers, he hadn't seen one since he was sent to Oulu.

The men agreed to help one another. They debated how long he should subscribe to the *Northern News* for, and concluded that one year would probably be a waste of money, since the hermit's life was unsettled at present.

Huttunen gave the postman the money for a quarterly subscription and Piittisjärvi promised to send off the form as soon as he got to the village.

Huttunen wrote a short letter to Sanelma Käyrämö. He found the bank's letter in his wallet to use for paper, but he didn't have a pen. He made do with a stick dipped in soot.

Huttunen spread out Ervinen's maps in front of his associate. They discussed where the hermit should build his new camp and set up the moonshine apparatus, and decided on a little ridge overlooking the Puukko, bordering the marsh, about a mile and a half from the source of the stream. Huttunen had found it that morning when he had gone fishing. He thought it was safer than the hill where they were now brewing up their nectar. The men also chose where Piittisjärvi would put Huttunen's letterbox. He could come and collect his mail three times a week. On the Lord's Day, and sometimes even during the week as well, Piittisjärvi would come and drink in the camp.

'I'll deliver straight to your door on Sundays, so don't bother going all the way to the letterbox for the Saturday papers.'

Huttunen asked Piittisjärvi to get him some salt, sugar, coffee and smoked bacon, and of course tobacco, and gave him money for it all.

After eating, the postman had to set off for the village because it was a delivery day. Washing his soot-streaked face in the stream and gargling to get rid of the worst fumes, he told Huttunen what to do if the mash over-heated or if, for one reason or another, the distillate stopped flowing.

'The worst thing is to let the mash boil away completely. It happened to me in the summer of 1939. My wife had died the autumn before and I was thinking how I was going to pass the time. The mash stuck to the bottom.

I was cleaning that tub for days. Everyone who drank that burnt batch was ill, one guy nearly died. And then when the Winter War broke out that autumn, he went and died in the first week anyway.'

Leaving Huttunen in charge, Piittisjärvi set off, tripping lightly across the marsh. He sauntered through the forest whistling, went straight to the post office, and before he did anything else, took out a three-month newspaper subscription for Huttunen. To be on the safe side, he put it in his name.

When he had finished his rounds that evening, Piittisjärvi went home to pick up a saw, a hammer, some nails, a few bits of board and a piece of laminated cardboard. He stowed them in his saddlebags and cycled to the deserted stretch of forest past the station where he had agreed with Huttunen to put up the letterbox. He chose a sturdy pine and set to work.

Progress was swift in the hands of a master. Piittisjärvi started with the frame, nailed on the boards, fixed the box to the tree and, with a knife, cut out a rectangle of laminated card the size of the lid to make it watertight. 'It's not such a great loss if the *Northern News* gets wet, but, when it comes to valuable mail, any negligence is unforgivable.'

To secure the lid, Piittisjärvi cut two strips of leather from the surplus length of his belt. There was room to cut plenty more. The postman thought sadly that he'd bought the belt in Kemi for his engagement. He was a brawny fellow in those days. But ever since his wife had died, he'd been gradually putting in new holes.

'Hilda always took good care of me when she was alive,' Piittisjärvi remembered, a lump forming in his scrawny throat.

The letterbox was ready; now it just needed to be painted. The postman wondered if it was sensible painting it the Post & Telegraph Office's regulation yellow. It may have been hidden from the road for the moment, but in the winter the official colour might give it away. Piittisjärvi decided to leave the wood bare, even though he had always hated delivering mail to shabby, neglected letterboxes. Once, drunk, he had taken Siponen to task after dropping off a bundle of letters in his miserable little pigeonhole, 'You could at least paint your letterbox, a big-shot farmer like you. It's like chucking the paper into a rabbit hutch. Not that it would matter where anyone bloody tossed your shrew's copies of *New Romance*.'

Piittisjärvi did however carve the post's symbol, the bugle, on the front of the letterbox and below it the owner's name: GUNNAR HUTTUNEN. Finally he dropped a copy of the *Northern News*, which he had brought with him, into the box, as if to inaugurate his creation.

'Now Kunnari can come and get his mail,' he thought to himself with satisfaction.

CHAPTER 29

The hermit once again had to set about building a new camp. He moved his things and Piittisjärvi's equipment to the foot of the little sandy ridge by Puukko Brook, which he christened 'Sandbank Camp'. He immediately rigged up a shelter, followed by the postman's still. He dug an oven in the lichen-covered slope and a bigger space a little further off where he put his tools, rucksack, fishing gear and rifle. Then he got down to distilling the firewater.

After the first distillation, Huttunen had collected twenty or so pints of foul-smelling liquor in the milk churn. He calculated that if he distilled it a second time, he would still have twelve. The hermit knew that if Piittisjärvi had done the boiling himself, he would have drunk the moonshine without bothering to clarify it further. But a sober, capable man was in charge now, and Huttunen boiled the brew a second time. He ended up with a good ten pints of alcohol as clear as the ice on an autumn lake and as strong as Ervinen's rectified spirit. He took a sip. It scalded the roof of his mouth; he spat out the stuff in disgust.

I'd better not drink, otherwise I'll go out of my mind again.

Huttunen hid the churn of firewater in a waterhole, dismantled the still and buried it in a thicket of firs on the banks of the stream. Then he threw his rifle over his shoulder, gathered up his fishing gear and set off to stock up on food. He headed northwest by compass, towards the woods where he had gone capercaillie shooting with Constable Portimo the previous winter. The familiar land-scape brought back happy memories: they had bagged plenty of birds that trip without even having a dog. Portimo's spitz had been left at home, because, having been trained to hunt bear, it wouldn't have crossed its mind to bark at capercaillie. If this had been a normal summer, Huttunen reflected, he'd be hunting with Portimo now, not trekking through the forest alone. The police constable wasn't doing what he'd expected either.

Portimo's wasted the best part of the summer chasing me. He must feel terrible having to hound a friend.

Huttunen had no difficulty finding a good place for game. He shot a couple of birds and on the way back caught several pounds of fish at the source of the stream. Before he reached his camp, he picked another basket of blueberries.

Life was good, but lonely. He didn't need to scour the forest; the birds were gutted and hanging from the trees, the fish were salting in birch bark creels deep in the cool moss. To pass the time, Huttunen decided to go and see if he had any mail. Would Piittisjärvi have had time to deliver his paper?

The hermit easily found the letterbox at the agreed spot, in the forest near the station. He circled around it first to check that it wasn't a trap, that there was no chance of an ambush. But as the wood seemed silent and deserted, he ventured closer. His name was carved on the front.

A rush of joy warmed the lonely man's heart: now he had a point of contact with the world, this crude grey box on the side of a pine. Piittisjärvi had done a good job.

But was there any mail inside? The hermit was afraid to open it. The disappointment if it were empty would be bitter in this forlorn place.

When Huttunen lifted the lid, he had the happy surprise of finding two newspapers and a thick envelope bearing his name in a female hand. He recognised the handwriting: the horticulture adviser Sanelma Käyrämö had sent him a letter.

The hermit retreated a few hundred yards from the letterbox into a dense fir thicket where he opened the envelope. It was a beautiful love letter. Huttunen read it, his face shining with happiness; his head hummed, the lines blurred as tears came into his eyes; his hands trembled and his heart pounded. He felt like howling for pure joy.

Included with the letter was a little leaflet, which bore the title NATIONAL INSTITUTE OF EDUCATION THROUGH THE MEDIUM OF THE POST: BUSINESS STUDIES.

Explaining her reasons for enclosing this brochure setting out the Institute's programme, Sanelma begged her beloved recipient 'not to throw it away, but to look it over and begin one of their correspondence courses' since Gunnar now had time on his hands and it was important never to remain idle and always try, even in difficult circumstances, to increase one's store of knowledge. When all was said and done, this was the only way that every Finn could achieve the personal happiness and success that would contribute to the wellbeing of the country as a whole.

Huttunen ran all the way back to his camp, reaching it in an hour and a half, even though it was almost thirteen miles across the marshes. He dived into his hut and re-read Sanelma Käyrämö's love letter. He read every word of it over and over until he knew it by heart. Only then did he turn to the papers.

There was a lot of coverage of the Korean War. A complicated conflict was unfolding in the distant forests of Asia, which seemed over the summer to have turned into a war of positions. Huttunen remembered how the Americans, Koreans and Chinese had each by turns held the upper hand the previous winter. Now the front had stabilised along the 38th Parallel and the Soviet Union was pushing for the start of negotiations prior to a ceasefire. One paper had a picture of an army jeep full of officers with artillery and high mountains in the background. The caption said UN troops were constantly patrolling supply routes to guard against ambushes. The flag fluttering on the jeep's bumper oddly enough, however, was a United States one. Huttunen hoped that the different sides would reach an agreement. As soon as there was peace, the price of wood would tumble in Finland. Then at least the big-shot farmers, Siponen and Vittavaara in particular, wouldn't be able to get rich on Korean blood anymore.

People were starting to talk about the Olympic Games. Apparently they were going to be held the following summer in Helsinki. In his day, Huttunen had cleared 12.8 feet in the pole vault using a pole made of poplar, and he had seriously thought of competing. But then the Winter War had broken out and the Helsinki Games had had to be cancelled. Huttunen didn't have a chance of watching the Games now, even though the war was over. He'd be caught the minute he tried to leave the woods.

The paper reported that the Soviets were planning to take part in the Olympics for the first time. Why not, Huttunen thought. They'd probably have some good hammer throwers, judging by how far they could throw grenades on the Svir.

They'll sweep the board in the marathon, but the Finnish soldier is quicker on a bicycle. If they have cycling events, that is.

After reading the newspapers, Huttunen studied the brochure for the Institute of Education through the Medium of the Post. The system's merits were praised

213

from every angle. The claim was advanced that *'an enterprising, well organised businessman or businesswoman can find a good position quicker and more easily than most people working in other fields'*.

Huttunen thought of his own trade of miller. It was quite true that business was an easier way to earn one's crust than working the aged Suukoski mill, when, given that frosts could take everything, you couldn't even be sure there'd be good grain to mill every year. Luckily he could make a living from the shingle saw, but he couldn't expand. There was no money to start a sawmill. And people were talking about electric mills now where one could mill one's grain without having to pay for water rights. In all these respects, there was a case to be made for a change of profession. But if the hermit thought clearly about his situation for a moment, how could he get a job in business when, as an outlaw, he daren't even start up his own mill?

On the other hand, Huttunen saw that studying could be a useful pastime. The Institute explained that the tuition was carried out entirely by correspondence: *'Anyone who has attended primary school can take our courses, whatever their place of residence, their age and the time available to them. It is enough for them to live in a place where the post is regularly delivered and to study when it suits them and they have the time.'*

Such a form of teaching seemed to have been conceived specifically for the life Huttunen was now leading. What did it matter where he was studying, the forest or the mill? Piittisjärvi delivered his mail to the forest; there was no reason to tell that to the gentlemen of the Institute.

Huttunen ate half a black grouse with cranberries for his supper. Then he threw himself on his bed of fir needles, his rifle within reach. Before falling asleep, he read the horticulture adviser's letter again. Perhaps my life will still work itself out, if Sanelma carries on sending me such passionate letters, Huttunen thought hopefully, before drifting off to sleep amid a smell of sap from the fir branches.

CHAPTER 30

On Sunday the hermit of Sandbank Camp received a visit. Postman Piittisjärvi and the horticulture adviser Sanelma Käyrämö came to pay their respects. The little postman led the way, carrying a heavy bag on his back, surrounded by a swarm of mosquitoes, and the 4H adviser followed, pink-cheeked and blooming. They were both exhausted from their long trek – the adviser's head was spinning – but when she saw Huttunen, all her tiredness evaporated. She threw her arms round the hermit's neck, and he suddenly felt so wonderful that he couldn't help howling with happiness.

Piittisjärvi waited impatiently for the embracing and howling to finish. Then he gave a semi-official cough and inquired, 'Any luck with the brewing, Kunnari?'

Huttunen led the man to the icy water hole and drew the churn of homebrew up from its depths; he opened the lid and gave Piittisjärvi a sniff. The postman jammed his little head in as far as it could go. The vessel echoed with a joyous whooping. Beside himself with gratitude, Piittisjärvi exclaimed that he had some things for Huttunen that were almost as precious.

'Come and tick them off the list!'

They went back to the camp where Sanelma Käyrämö was making coffee. Piittisjärvi emptied the contents of his bag onto the floor of the hut. There was everything Huttunen could need: big bags of salt and sugar, a packet of coffee, a sack of flour, semolina, two pounds of bacon, four pounds of butter . . . last to roll onto the spruce needles were a head of cabbage, several bunches of carrots, turnips, pea pods, beetroot, celery, Brussel sprouts and five or six pounds of new potatoes!

Huttunen looked tenderly at Sanelma Käyrämö who gave him a shy, happy smile.

'Think about cooking those vegetables, Gunnar. They're best grated. All of them come from your garden, except the cabbage and the celery.'

'How can I thank you?' Huttunen stammered. He looked fondly at Piittisjaärvi's frail silhouette and the mound of provisions he had carried through the forest from the village. 'You must have worked up quite a sweat carrying all that, Postman.'

Piittisjärvi played down his labours in a manly way.

'What's a sack, a few cabbages . . . Remember the day I ran from the eastern forests to Puukko Hill with my still? *That* was hard work. If it hadn't been my mash,

I would have left it in Reutu woods under the police chief's nose, believe me.'

The bag's pockets contained writing paper and envelopes, a pencil and rubber, a pencil sharpener, a ruler, notebooks, a pad and a variety of books, including Institute of Education through the Medium of the Post course books. Huttunen thanked his guests at length as he transferred their gifts to his rucksack. He had mail as well: the *Northern News* and a bill from Kemi Hardware for the driving belt he'd ordered in the spring. Quite expensive, Huttunen noted. He dropped the bill in the fire.

'I think I'm going to leave you two lovebirds,' Piittisjärvi announced, the soul of consideration since he was hoping to get away for a *tête-à-tête* with his churn. But the water was boiling and the postman had to wait to attend to his business. Sanelma Käyrämö opened the packet of coffee and poured a generous measure into the pot. Piittisjärvi downed his cup in one and did not have another. With steam filtering from his mouth, he left the hut and promised not to return for at least two hours.

'You do what you like, I won't be around to see.'

That was a happy Sunday. A cool, late summer breeze drove the mosquitoes down in the marshes, away from the lichen-covered ridge. The sun shone, Puukko Brook burbled quietly, a heady smell of peat hung in the air. The horticulture adviser and Huttunen talked constantly, envisaging Huttunen's future, sighing and kissing by turns. The hermit would have liked to go further but Sanelma Käyrämö stopped him. He realised she was afraid of getting pregnant and giving birth to a mentally disturbed baby. Sanelma Käyrämö said that she wanted to marry Huttunen later, when the situation was clearer. But she didn't dare have a child now. She envisaged having one with Huttunen in the future, when he was cured ... She would do anything to help Gunnar to recover from his illness. Then they could have as many children as they liked. But if his condition did not improve, she couldn't risk it.

'We can adopt a child, or two. We'll choose healthy babies. You can get them straight from Kemi maternity and you don't even have to pay the mothers. They're so poor they can't feed their children themselves.'

Huttunen tried to understand her fears. It would be truly horrible to be categorised as mad the minute you were born ... The hermit made plans to sell the mill. He decided to write to Happola in Oulu. Perhaps he could arrange the sale after all. Summer was nearly over. He wondered if Happola had got out of hospital, now ten years had passed since the start of the War of Continuation when he had gone in.

Huttunen dictated a letter to Sanelma for Happola. They stuck a stamp on the envelope. He gave Happola *carte blanche* to deal with the affair.

In the afternoon they ate. Sanelma Käyrämö prepared vegetable soup. They made open sandwiches with bacon and lettuce and the adviser set out grated vegetables and stewed berries on little birch bark dishes.

'Absolutely delicious,' the two men said. Flushed with pleasure, Sanelma Käyrämö pushed her curls off her forehead every now and then. Huttunen couldn't take his eyes off the young woman; he was so in love with her it hurt. He found it almost impossible to stay sitting down and, with love alone bringing him to his feet, would have liked to walk round and round the fire.

After the meal, the guests had to set off for the village, because it was a long way back and Piittisjärvi was spectacularly drunk. Huttunen went with them. Luckily they didn't have much to carry, but Sanelma Käyrämö found it tiring all the same, since she wasn't used to great hikes through the forest. Piittisjärvi was also tired, but for different reasons. Huttunen walked the last part of the way in the middle, supporting both his guests. Piittisjärvi chatted and laughed, while the adviser leant languorously into Huttunen. They reached the main road in this order, and Huttunen and Sanelma Käyrämö tenderly said their farewells. Both promised to write. Piittisjärvi swore he would deliver their letters free of charge.

'Why put them in the post, stamp them for nothing? No need to lick any stamps, the sort of postman I am, I won't make any fuss ... I'll turn a blind eye. The Telegraph isn't going to fly off the handle just because Kunnari doesn't stick a stamp on all his envelopes!'

When he was alone, Huttunen returned to the banks of the Kemijoki, took a boat and crossed the river. Making his way through the eastern forest, he reached Mount Reutu, where he settled down to wait for nightfall. On the stroke of midnight, Huttunen started howling. He called out in a high, powerful voice so everyone in the village would hear him. Then he stopped for a cigarette, and thought that they would come looking for him on Mount Reutu and along the Sivakka after this fresh bout of howling.

You've got to know how to howl to give yourself an escape route.

Finishing his cigarette, Huttunen began again: long, plaintive wails interspersed with a low, menacing snarling, like a hunted animal. He carried on until he was out of breath and sated. It was a delight, really, after all this time being unable to howl.

Having bayed his fill, Huttunen fell silent to listen to the results. The village dogs had heard his cry; a chorus of barking echoed from all parts. No one in the vicinity would get a wink of sleep that night.

His task accomplished, Huttunen left Mount Reutu. He did not reach his camp west of the Kemijoki until the early hours of the morning. Lying down to sleep in his hut, Huttunen thought it was a tough life when you had to trek dozens of miles, steal a boat twice, row across the Kemijoki twice – and all for what? Rushing around all night just to have a howl?

CHAPTER 31

The weather turned cool and rainy. Confined to the hut, his hermit's existence began to weigh on Huttunen. The nights were cold and misty, the days deathly dull. The only good thing about the change in the weather was that the fish were biting. This was the best season for fishing, the end of summer. But Huttunen didn't have any barrels to salt his catch, so he couldn't even spend his time on the river.

As the rain set in, the hut's roof began to spring leaks. To improve matters, Huttunen tore off long hoops of bark from stout birches and laid them on the shelter like shingles on the roof of a barn. No water got in after that and, since he had decided to keep a little fire going all day in the hut, Huttunen was much more cosy. But time dragged terribly. Thinking for hours on end wasn't very entertaining, especially when most of one's thoughts were crazy.

Huttunen immersed himself in the books the horticulture adviser had bought him, including the publications
of the Institute of Education through the Medium of
the Post. He started with a medical work by a certain
H. Fabritius, *Nervousness and Nervous Illnesses*. It was
hailed on the dust jacket as the most remarkable book ever
written on the subject in Finland. Interested, Huttunen
looked for an explanation of his own mental illness. Several
descriptions initially seemed to correspond to his case.
He recognised himself in the chapter 'Hypersensitive and
easily irritated people', for instance. The one on sexual
problems caused by nervous illnesses, on the other hand,
didn't spark any recognition. His sexual organs were in
perfect working order! The only obstacle to his desires
was the horticulture adviser Sanelma Käyrämö's fear of
having a mad baby.

The book detailed case histories of patients suffering
from 'obsession, otherwise known as psychasthenic
neurosis'. Huttunen had to admit that he displayed some
of the symptoms mentioned but he still didn't feel he was
really psychasthenic. As a whole, the book failed to live
up to its reader's expectations, who finished it still uncertain as to exactly what illness he suffered from. That apart,
however, Huttunen found the book interesting, even
amusing. He particularly enjoyed the descriptions of the
psychopaths. Case 14 struck him as one of the funniest.

A middle-aged man who had never left Germany
used to travel the country giving lectures. He claimed

to have been born in South Africa, in Pretoria, the capital of the Transvaal. He had performed legendary feats during the Boer War, notably fighting in forty-two battles, and President Krüger had awarded him a baronetcy in recognition of his services. At the lectures, he would sell postcards of himself in military uniform (ill. 3).

In the photograph, the man was wearing a splendid officer's uniform. A likeable-looking fellow who Huttunen warmed to immediately. The hermit was overwhelmed with rage when he read how the Germans had treated this kindred spirit. Apparently 'the police took an interest in the man's activities and sent him to be examined in a psychiatric hospital where he was certified as a psychopath of the mythomanic, adventurer type'.

Fabritius analysed the case from a Finnish point of view. He noted that the man 'could not be considered a criminal, but society was not able to allow one of its members to earn his living giving lectures which were just hot air, even if they were fascinating and apparently entertained his audiences'.

Incandescent, Huttunen flung the book into the corner. He could imagine the ordeal the poor man had suffered in a German asylum in such a primitive era. German hospitals would have been far grimmer than the madhouse at Oulu, which was a living hell as it was.

Huttunen threw himself into studying. The correspondence course began with written expression; he did the exercises, read the examples of principal and subordinate propositions and gazed in amazement at certain instances of juxtaposition and conjunction:

Work triumphs over circumstance; work precludes
sleep.
We will go for a long hike and spend all day in
the forest.
We will only go if it's hot.

The sentences' content interested him more than their grammatical construction. He thought of his long hikes and reflected with irritation that he would have to stay all summer in the forest, no matter how cold it got. Police Chief Jaatila had seen to that.

Huttunen familiarised himself with the '*eng*', or '*äng*', sound. It tickled him that grown men actually bothered making rules about something so obvious. The chapter on the glottal occlusive, or aspiration, was less enigmatic. He amused himself talking without a glottal stop for a moment. Everything he said sent him into hysterics. It was lucky no one could hear.

Law and business practices appealed to him much more than written expression. He started with the manual Sanelma Käyrämö had got him, which was written by I. V. Kaitila and Esa Kaitila. Any relation? Married perhaps?

The style was dry but things were explained concisely and in an easily comprehensible way. According to the correspondence course, one need only read the first twenty pages to start with but, as there was barely any let-up in the rain, Huttunen devoured the whole book from cover to cover. Then he moved on to the exercises.

One question compared wholesale and retail practices. Huttunen thought of the shopkeeper Tervola. At the end of his answer, he added, 'In our village the retailer Tervola refuses to sell food to the mentally ill unless he is threatened with an axe. It would be easier getting served in a wholesaler than it is in his shop.'

Why doesn't the Bank of Finland pay interest on deposits?

Another interesting question. Huttunen spoke of the role of the central bank, as the Kaitilas had explained it, and almost went on to mention the bank manager Huhtamoinen, who did not pay all savers their interest, or even their principal, and thus behaved even more despotically than the Bank of Finland, but eventually he decided against it. What interest were Huttunen's money problems to the Institute of Education through the Medium of the Post? The main thing at the moment was studying, not Huhtamoinen's banking practices.

What is a documentary credit? What is a bond?

Huttunen was amused and intrigued by business terminology. He found it easy to remember and regretted not having done business studies when he was younger. Not only was the subject surprisingly easy, it could be useful too. If a rich businessman began howling, for instance, he might be forgiven more readily than a miller.

Anyway, he could still learn at his age.

Huttunen gleefully imagined finishing his business studies and receiving the Institute's diploma. It should be before Christmas, the lessons seemed easy enough. When he had completed his course in the forest, it would be hard for people to think of him just as a lunatic anymore. If he paid the police chief a few fines for howling, perhaps he could be the stockman at a wholesaler's one day! He could even run a mill as well, if there was one nearby, why not?

Then Huttunen remembered he couldn't actually get a diploma himself. As a precaution, the courses had been put in the postman Piittisjärvi's name, so the certificate would obviously be in his name too. Huttunen would just have the knowledge of the subject, which did not seem a great deal without any official recognition.

On the other hand, if one considered the matter from Piittisjärvi's point of view, the postman stood to benefit considerably from his studies. The chap just had to carry on delivering Huttunen's letters and sucking away on his homebrew and, next thing he knew, he'd have a diploma in business studies. If he handled things right, he could zip up the postal hierarchy and be appointed village postmaster. The present incumbent didn't have any qualifications, so people said. Huttunen tried to imagine Piittisjärvi in charge of the post office, enthroned behind a huge desk, his glasses perched on the tip of his nose, occasionally applying one of a panoply of official stamps to a registered letter.

Pleased with the image, the hermit immersed himself in the Kaitilas' manual again.

What does it matter which of us goes up in the world, Piittisjärvi or me, he thought, testing himself on rediscount.

On Friday, the weather grew a little warmer and it stopped raining. Huttunen put his assignments in an envelope, stamped it and wrote a letter to the horticulture adviser. Then he went to take his correspondence to his forest letterbox. There should be two or three editions of the *Northern News* waiting for him, and who knew what else? Word from Sanelma Käyrämö?

Night was falling when Huttunen reached his letterbox. He approached warily, but no one was spying on him; the place was still a secret. He found the newspapers and a letter from Sanelma. She declared ardent love for Huttunen and said that another huge search party had gone looking for him east of the Kemijoki. The chief of police had apparently ranted and raved and called Constable Portimo every name under the sun for having failed to catch Huttunen all summer.

There was an article in the *Northern News* about the provincial athletics championships that would be taking place the following Sunday on the village sports ground. No less than the provincial governor, who was on a tour of inspection of the district, had promised to attend. The paper listed the championship's and the governor's programmes.

Huttunen decided that he'd attend the championships as well. Perhaps he could watch the events from the top of a hill? Climb a tree and admire the athletes' feats through

Ervinen's binoculars. The loudspeaker announcements wouldn't carry very far, but that didn't matter too much. The main thing was to see the event and the governor.

No need to buy a ticket this way either.

CHAPTER 32

Huttunen left Sandbank Camp in the early hours of Sunday morning so as to get to the village before its inhabitants awoke. He stole another boat again on the banks of the Kemijoki and rowed across the river. The village was asleep. The air was cool, almost autumnal, and it was still dark. Huttunen began looking for a suitable vantage point from which to watch the provincial athletic championships without being discovered.

There were two tall hills near the village. Neither suited Huttunen's purposes, however, because all one could see from one were the wooden tiles and steeple of the new church, while the tower where the firemen dried their hoses blocked the view from the other. A third possibility was to watch the championships from Mount Reutu, but it was too far away – even Ervinen's binoculars wouldn't be strong enough to follow the action.

The best thing would have been to go up the firemen's tower but that was out of the question, the head of the council's road maintenance department lived on the ground floor. Which left only the bell tower of the new church. Why not give it a try?

Huttunen crept stealthily through the deserted church-yard and tried the church doors. All locked. Behind the sacristy, there was a door leading to the cellar. It was also locked but the cellar window swung open when Huttunen pushed it. He squeezed through the little window into the cellar, and shut it behind him.

The basement was dreary and dark and smelled of leaf mould. Lighting a match, Huttunen saw a large room with an earth floor. Was this where they kept the communion wine? Was he about to bump into a mound of dessicated thighbones and shinbones of the long dead? Huttunen lit a few matches without being able to see any bottles or a trace of a skeleton. There was, on the other hand, a big pile of mossy bricks, a wheelbarrow and a cement mixer.

So, this is where the church stores its building materials. Come to think of it, it's probably unlikely anyone has been buried here, the church was only built at the start of the century.

The door at the top of the cellar stairs was open. Huttunen found himself in the sacristy. He had no problem passing from there to the huge nave of the church. The walls were covered with blue-grey panelling. Despite the gloom, one could see the paint was flaked and cracked, with big bare patches. In their delusions of grandeur, the canton's farmers had built a vast building, which their sons were now failing to maintain. Whether this was through lack of faith or money, Huttunen didn't know.

He couldn't resist going up to the pulpit briefly. He struck a pastor's pose and uttered a rousing howl. The echo between the high walls of the church was so loud that Huttunen took fright and hurried back down again. He went up to the gallery. Behind the organ, a spiral staircase led to the bell tower.

The staircase made seven complete turns before it reached the belfry, a small hexagonal room with two bells hanging from the roof, one big and one small. Round windows opened on its six sides. They were without panes, which stood to reason, since they would have muffled the sound of the bells. Looking out of one of them at the ground, Huttunen's head spun, it was so high up.

From the vertiginous heights of the bell tower, the view stretched over the village and the blue-tinged mountains in the distance. The sports ground lay in the foreground, offered up, as it were, on a plate to the spectator. One could follow all the disciplines at a glance. Huttunen couldn't have found a better seat if he'd tried. He trained his binoculars on the sandy running track. As far as he was concerned, the championships could begin right now.

It had grown light, at last, and the time had slowly crept towards ten o'clock. The meet would be starting in just over an hour. The hermit studied the programme he'd cut out of the *Northern News*. The field events were straight after the governor's speech, and proceedings would culminate with the track events: 3000 metres, 400 metres hurdles and 100 metres. That was Huttunen's speciality, the 400-metre hurdles. On the Svir front during the war, he had won the divisional championship. The prize had been five days' leave, which he had spent in Sortavala, losing his spiked running shoes and catching a dose of crabs in the process.

Voices sounded below, in the churchyard. The pastor was walking up the path with the verger. It was then that Huttunen remembered that it was a Sunday and time for the morning service. Still, it didn't matter. He was safe in the belfry; there was nothing he needed from the church. He'd be able to hear the hymns; maybe he'd even join in the singing to pass the time. And then, straight after the service, the main attraction would begin – the provincial athletics championships.

Sounds echoed up from the church. Doors banged, the floor creaked. The sexton played a few notes on the organ. Then Huttunen thought he could hear footsteps on the stairs leading to the bell tower. The pastor? What on earth could he want in the bell tower? Huttunen went to the top of the staircase and listened. No doubt about it: someone was on their way up.

Then the penny suddenly dropped. It was the verger coming to ring the bells, of course!

The situation was critical. There was nowhere to hide in the little room. The bell ringer's footsteps were coming closer.

Don't even think of jumping out of the window.

The farmhand Launola climbed the last few steps, and as he got to the door, completely off his guard, Huttunen punched him in the head. Launola almost fell down the stairs, but Huttunen managed to catch him, grab him under the arms and drag him over to the bells. The farm-hand was unconscious but breathing steadily. Huttunen felt his heartbeat; he wasn't seriously hurt. Huttunen tied his hands behind his back with his belt. Then he took off the farmhand's shirt and made it into a gag. Once Launola couldn't move or make a sound, Huttunen propped him up by a window to revive him. In the morning breeze, the farmhand quickly came round.

'You're the verger now, are you?' Huttunen whispered. Launola nodded, terrified.

'Where's the real verger?'

The farmhand mimed someone being ill.

'So you've come to ring the bells?'

His prisoner nodded.

Huttunen took out his watch. Lord, the service would be starting any minute! It was time to ring the bells. He couldn't leave it to Launola; he'd be bound to work out some way to raise the alarm. The congregation would rush to the bell tower to see what danger the verger's replacement was in. Huttunen decided that, this Sunday, he would have to ring the church bells himself.

He tried to remember the bells' usual rhythm. Long pauses, that was all he could remember. Did you have to play a particular tune? Huttunen hadn't the slightest idea.

The best thing would just be to keep time. Huttunen grabbed the rope of the little bell and gave it a brisk yank. The bell moved a little, swinging above the horizontal before returning to its original position. Huttunen pulled it again: the bell soared to the top of its trajectory and gave an ear-splitting peal as it fell. With the other hand, Huttunen hauled harder on the rope tied to the clapper of the big bell. It produced an even more fearsome noise. Huttunen pulled the ropes in time, creating a deafening racket.

This is a pretty decent invitation to God-fearing folk to get themselves to church, isn't it?

Huttunen hesitated. How long should he go on for? Ten minutes? More? The ringing was hard work, plus he had to keep an eye on Launola who was sitting by the window, racking his brains as to how to escape. Huttunen tugged away, bathed in sweat; the thunderous booming made the church tremble. He imagined the distances those infernal peals would carry, the remoteness of the hamlets they would reach. He wouldn't be surprised if the people of Rovaniemi could hear how Christendom was called to worship God in this pious canton.

Despite the blur of his pumping arms, Huttunen managed to get a glimpse of his watch. It showed one minute to ten. He decided to stop at ten, that was prob-ably right; the pastor had to make his entrance at some point or another. The hermit's ears were already shot by the diabolical racket.

At ten o'clock, Huttunen let go of the bell ropes. The

little bell rang twice more, the big one once, and then a heavenly silence descended on the bell tower.

Moments later, a fervent hymn rose up from the church. The faithful hadn't noticed anything abnormal about Huttunen's ringing.

The pastor's sermon was inaudible in the belfry but even Huttunen joined in the final psalm. Then the service was over and the worshippers left the church to go straight to the sports ground. There had been no collection that Sunday, the verger being off sick and his replacement tied up in the bell tower, but the congregation didn't seem to be complaining. Huttunen felt a pang of remorse: thanks to him, the children of more than one heathen country would be deprived of the money the parish would otherwise have sent for their evangelisation. He promised that when he was a rich businessman, he would reimburse the parish and its missions.

The sports ground's loudspeakers began blaring. Huttunen went to a window and raised Ervinen's binoculars to his eyes. He saw a group of competitors in tracksuits and hundreds of spectators. On the far side of the stadium, by the finishing line, a sort of enclosure had been built with a wooden fence, in which a few chairs had been set out. The governor was in the front row surrounded by local dignitaries: the police chief, the president of the municipal council, Dr Ervinen, the pastor, and a few rich farmers, including Vittavaara and Siponen. The former had come with his wife; the latter was enjoying the event alone.

Huttunen searched for Sanelma Käyrämö with his binoculars. He scanned the crowd painstakingly until at last he spotted the adviser, off to one side slightly, on a small hill planted with pines near the churchyard. She was with a group of young women dressed like her in scarves and colourful skirts. Huttunen was so happy to see Sanelma that he almost howled in greeting.

The governor took the microphone. The angle of the loudspeakers meant that his speech was heard twice in the bell tower. It sounded as if he was imitating himself. He emphasised the role of sport in developing moral fibre and urged his fellow citizens to compete at every possible opportunity. Speaking of the reparations that Finland had been required to pay in kind, he described their imbursement as an extraordinary sporting feat on the part of an entire nation.

'If the train carrying that sum had been a second, or even a tenth of a second, late reaching the border, the payee would have instantly demanded exorbitant damages. Let this be a concrete example to our youth that there can be never be any excuse for shilly-shallying at the finish line.'

The governor moved on to the Olympic Games that were to take place the following summer in Helsinki. He trusted that the canton's sportsmen and sportswomen would compete and return to Lapland festooned with gold and silver medals.

After the speech, the athletics started. The farmhand Launola dragged himself over to Huttunen's side where he conveyed by gestures that he'd like to watch the competition. Despite disliking the man, Huttunen made room for him at the window. The wretched part-time verger gratefully began watching the throwing disciplines. At that moment a fellow from Kanto Lake was taking his run up in the javelin. He let fly, and the projectile soared effortlessly into the governor's enclosure. He was instantly disqualified, despite being in the lead.

The pole-vaulters used modern bamboo poles. Huttunen was looking forward to some good results but to his disappointment, the winner only managed 11.3 feet. When the fellow was presented with his commemorative spoon, Huttunen couldn't help shouting from the top of the bell tower, 'Clumsy oaf!'

The cry reverberated across the sports ground. The crowd and the guests of honour looked up at the heavens whence the voice seemed to have fallen. Two crows were clumsily flying overhead at that moment, coming from the churchyard, and they cawed balefully as they flapped past. The governor and the spectators turned their attention back to the events.

Huttunen avidly watched the 400-metre hurdles. There were only three runners, not including the *Northern News* photographer who ran alongside taking pictures, his raincoat flapping. Huttunen actually thought he'd won the hard-fought race because the winner hit his knee so badly on the last hurdle that he had to be taken to Dr Ervinen in the VIP enclosure. Ervinen bowed politely to the governor, pulled down the runner's tracksuit bottoms and slapped his knee with the flat of his hand. A scream of agony rent the air.

Huttunen and Launola watched the championships from start to finish, Huttunen's binoculars straying repeatedly from the winning athletes to the horticulture adviser Sanelma Käyrämö, whose blonde hair fluttered ravishingly in the late summer breeze.

CHAPTER 33

After his public duties were over, the governor was invited to Police Chief Jaatila's house. The sauna on the banks of the Kemijoki had been heated in his honour and a light meal laid out on the veranda with coffee. Besides the chief of police, the governor's retinue consisted of Dr Ervinen, the pastor, the president of the municipal council and the bank manager Huhtamoinen. The schoolteacher hadn't been invited but Vittavaara was there; he owned a great deal of land, after all, and the Korean situation had made him rich.

They talked about the Korean War, the Olympic Games, war reparations, the industrialisation of Lapland and the spread of logging, finally, to public land.

'Our people will get back on their feet,' declared the governor, emerging naked from the chilly waters of the Kemijoki.

When the distinguished guests had come out of the sauna and were assembled in the chief of police's living room, a small bottle of cognac was opened and a toast drunk. Only one, since the governor was unfortunately on the abstemious side.

'*A propos* . . .' the governor began. 'Word has reached Rovaniemi that you've got a madman around here who refuses to go quietly and get treatment at Oulu mental hospital. They say his favourite pastime is to howl all night.'

The chief of police cleared his throat. Seeking to play down the problem, he pointed out that you found people who were not quite right in the head everywhere, in every village.

Ervinen and Vittavaara, however, their cheeks flushed from the cognac, launched into a description of the miller Huttunen's activities for the governor's benefit. They listed all his transgressions in detail, and insisted the man was armed and dangerous, and terrorising the whole village. No one could do anything about him.

Jaatila tried to minimise the extent of the affair. The man wasn't really dangerous, he stressed, just a bit crazy and simple-minded; he wasn't worth taking seriously.

'In the final analysis, I'd describe the miller Huttunen as an oddball . . . He's unstable, certainly, but harmless and naturally easygoing.'

But the governor had heard enough.

'It is totally unacceptable that an armed, mentally disturbed and, it would seem, extremely dangerous individual should be allowed to roam the forests of my province at will. Chief of Police Jaatila! You must step up your searches. This man must be sent to hospital without delay. Society has specifically allocated places for such individuals.'

At that moment, a distant, mournful howling came from the direction of Mount Reutu. The living-room window was half open; the governor opened it fully to be able to hear better. His face lit up with excitement.

'A wolf? Isn't that the call of a wolf?'

The chief of police went over, pretended to listen and said as he tried to shut the window, 'Yes, of course, a wolf . . . a lone wolf that must have crossed the border. Harmless at this time of year.'

The governor stopped him shutting the window. He said it was the first time he had heard a wolf howling in the wild.

'This is one of the happiest days of my life! Pour me another drop of cognac, Chief of Police, just this once!'

Ervinen broke the spell by remarking venomously, 'It's not a wolf. I know my patient's voice. That's the miller Huttunen howling out there.'

'He's always yelped like that,' confirmed Vittavaara. 'It's definitely Huttunen and not a wolf. You must have recognised him too, Jaatila.'

The chief of police had to admit that if he listened more closely, yes, perhaps it was Huttunen howling after all.

The governor exploded. This was utterly incredible: they were letting the man terrorise the canton with complete impunity. Why didn't they go and arrest him immediately?

The chief of police explained that it would be almost impossible to find the miller until the ground had become harder with the first frosts. It would require a lot of men, trained dogs and luck. There was only one constable in the canton, Portimo, who was not up to the task and had already let the former miller escape several times. For the moment, all they could do was let Huttunen howl. In autumn, when it started snowing, the chief of police would put an end to his yapping. But in the meantime there was nothing that could be done.

The governor was of a different opinion.

'I'm going to have the light infantry regiment of the Rovaniemi frontier division send you backup. They'll soon flush this lunatic out of the woods, I can assure you. If you're short of men and dogs, Police Chief Jaatila, I will personally see to that side of the matter.'

The window was closed. Coffee was poured for the governor. Police Chief Jaatila went and sat down, highly irritated. The way he did his job had just been sharply criticised, all thanks to that loudmouth Dr Ervinen, that imbecile Vittavaara . . . and of course the devil incarnate, Huttunen.

After a pause, the police chief suggested to the governor that they open peace talks with the miller Gunnar Huttunen and try to come to an agreement.

'Couldn't we grant this man an amnesty of some sort? We could get word to him saying he can come out of the forest, he won't blamed for the error of his ways, he won't even be taken straight to hospital ... I am sure if he returned to civilisation he would calm down. We could even demand a written promise from him not to howl within earshot of his fellow villagers. Our rural counsellor has given us to understand that she has been in contact with him. We could draw a veil over this whole lamentable affair.'

The governor thought the suggestion over, but decided against it.

'No. It's out of the question. We can amnesty a criminal, that's not a problem, but how can we do the same for a lunatic? It is not within the authorities' power. The situation is quite clear: the man must be taken to the psychiatric hospital where he belongs immediately. I will not allow a human being to howl in the woods of my province.'

There was a noise in the hall. The maid came in to tell the chief of police that someone called Launola wanted to talk to him. The police chief went into the hall to listen to the farmhand. In the living room, the governor made out the hermit Huttunen's name amid the shouting. He called in the chief of police and the farmhand.

'Tell us what you know about this Huttunen, young man.'

Launola bowed and began to explain that he had stood in for the verger of the parish who was ill.

'He's got emphysema and he's in bed because the medicine isn't doing any good and he hasn't got any money to go to any other doctor than . . . than . . . D–Dr Ervinen.'

'Get to the point, Launola,' Ervinen snapped. 'The governor's not interested in the verger's moth-eaten lungs.'

Launola said he had gone up to the bell tower of the church that morning to ring the bells. Huttunen had been waiting for him.

'Kunnari knocked me out and tied me up so I couldn't get away or make a sound. Then he rang the bells himself and after the service we watched the athletics. We even saw the governor, sir.'

Launola said Huttunen had kept him prisoner all day. The hermit hadn't left the bell tower with his victim until the evening. He had locked Launola in the church cellar. The farmhand had only just managed to escape through the window.

'That's all I had to tell you.'

He was allowed to go. When the door was shut behind him, the governor said severely, 'When a man behaves in such a fashion, with such brazen insolence, he must be arrested without delay, with the army's help if necessary. Can one imagine a more loathsome sacrilege: a madman ringing the bells in the House of the Lord!'

The governor opened the window of the living room again. Everyone listened in silence. But Mount Reutu was quiet. Huttunen was already on his way back to his camp west of the Kemijoki.

CHAPTER 34

Several days passed and then an old acquaintance appeared at Sandbank Camp: Happola. Huttunen was lying in the hut leafing through the Kaitilas' manual on marketing techniques, when the jays perched on his roof suddenly flew up, distracting him from his studies. Rifle in hand, the hermit awaited the intruder. When he recognised his fellow mental patient, he cried out, 'How did you get here so quickly?'

'You wrote to me, remember? What an expedition though! You live a bloody long way away these days. But your directions were pretty clear. It was only the letterbox that I had a bit of trouble finding.'

Happola looked extremely well and cheerful. He wore a new leather jacket and moleskin breeches, and, on his feet, a brand new pair of top boots. Huttunen put the kettle on and sliced some bread and bacon for his guest.

After drinking a first cup of coffee, Happola moved on to serious matters. He had left Oulu two days ago, he explained, spent the night in Kemi and then gone to the Suukoski mill.

'I was inspecting your mill yesterday and today.'

'And, what do you think? It's in good shape, don't you reckon?' Huttunen asked impatiently.

Happola acknowledged that it didn't look in bad shape at first sight. The building was freshly painted like new. The dam looked sturdy. The waterwheels appeared to be working. He was less sure about the driving belt. Huttunen said he'd ordered a new belt for the millstones in the spring. It was waiting at the station; the bill from Kemi Hardware just had to be paid.

'I don't know much about mills,' Happola added, 'but the stones for animal feed look newer than the ones for flour. And feed stones are barely cost-effective, as you know.'

'Don't worry, you'll be able to mill with those flour stones for years,' Huttunen insisted.

'The mill's main problem is that the logs at the base of the building have pretty bad woodworm. On the south side, three at least need to be replaced. There's rot at the end of the millrace as well. I tested the logs with my knife and it went in that far, or even more,' Happola reported, spreading the thumb and index finger of his left hand.

Huttunen admitted that two levels of logs on the wheel side would have to be replaced in the next couple of years, but as the mill was built on pillars, that wouldn't be difficult.

'You just have to lever up the base of the cabin, knock out the rotten logs and put in new ones. Then you just lower the building back into place. It's a day or two's work for a carpenter.'

'But it's going to affect the price. And don't forget that basically I don't need this mill, I've never worked in cereals.'

Nevertheless Happola made Huttunen an offer. The price was low; you could only have bought a little cabin, or two or three horses, with harness and plough, for the amount. But Huttunen couldn't refuse, because no one was going to make him a better offer in the depths of the forest. The men shook on it and the deal was done. Happola promised to send the money when his solicitor had authenticated the deed. He said he'd take care of the paperwork as soon as he got back to the village.

'I know a solicitor in Kemi. I just have to go over the mortgages, even though I trust you,' said Happola, who seemed delighted to have bought his first mill.

The men began talking about their time in hospital. Huttunen asked Happola how he had negotiated getting out. The man's features hardened.

'Christ! I wasted years of my life in that place. The last five years I spent inside were utterly pointless.' Happola explained that when his tenth year of mental illness had come to an end, he had gone straight to the doctor to announce that he was actually in perfect health. He told him the whole story. At first, no one believed him, but eventually, when he had told them about his double life in town, the hospital staff had to face facts. They had reluctantly declared him sane. However, they had imposed conditions on his release.

'Those imbeciles couldn't think of anything better to do than to call in the hospital administrator. He said that the institution didn't support people in good health for nothing. He thrust a bill for the last five years in my face and said that if I didn't pay it, I wouldn't get out. They bunged me in solitary confinement and threatened to put me in a straitjacket if I didn't cough up the money.'

Happola had asked what right they had to make him pay for five years in hospital, for his board and lodging in other words. The answer he got was that they would have demanded payment for all ten years if there weren't a statutory limitation concerning the services he'd used during the first five years. So Happola had paid the hospital for his treatment.

'The bill was absolutely criminal. What a cynical character, that administrator, what a skinflint! The meals were almost charged at restaurant prices, more or less – lunch, dinner and with a free health cure thrown in for every customer. And the room! As if I'd been swanning around in a hotel for five years! I had to stump up the full whack in one go. As soon as I got out, I went straight to my lawyer and it's going to court this winter. But I had to pay, so I paid.'

Happola resented it bitterly. He reminded Huttunen of the sort of food they served in the hospital.

'I ate their sludge for ten years. Maybe it wasn't your sort of thing, but I stuffed myself with it. At what a price, for Christ's sake!'

'It wasn't very good, it's true,' Huttunen acknowledged. He remembered the hospital's staple dish: a thick, lumpy porridge of oatmeal meant for cattle, that was generally cold by the time it got to the table. It wasn't unusual to find a full beard in one's bowl.

'That's how they fleece people in public institutions,' Happola grumbled. 'It's lucky the Korean War is still on. I sold forty acres of wood in Kiiminki and paid my hospital bill with the proceeds, and I've got enough left over to be able to help you with your mill. I've got a buyer in Kajaani; I'm not buying it just to leave it idle.'

Huttunen asked how their old roommates were.

'Still the same,' Happola said, shaking his head. 'Except that Rahkonen died at the start of July. He was the guy who sat all day in the same place, frowning. One day he died without a word; he fell over, just like that. A few days later, they brought us a slightly cheerier loopy loo instead, the sort who laugh at anything. Do you remember the skinny lad? He took your escape very badly, the poor boy. For weeks he was asking when you were coming back. Oh yes, remember the cleaning lady who made such a racket? She was moved to the women's wing, but when she started her usual complaining, the la-las grabbed her and beat the daylights out of her. They gave her a broken leg and now she's with the deaconesses. It's broken so badly she won't be back before Christmas. We got a new cleaner, a man. Lazy bugger. He didn't say anything, but he didn't do anything either.'

'What about the doctor?'

Happola said that the duty doctor was still cleaning his specs, same as ever.

'He hit the roof when I told him that I was sane and healthy. He began yelling and bawling and only calmed down when the orderlies came and threatened to put him in a straitjacket. He took it hard. You can understand, I suppose, when you've treated someone for ten years thinking they're mad and then they just turn up and say "Bye, I'm off now".'

'That doctor was ill himself.'

'You're telling me. The craziest bloody doctor in Finland.'

Huttunen showed Happola his camp, the gear he'd taken from Ervinen, the rifle and Piittisjärvi's still. He talked about his days, how he spent his time. In the circumstances, he said, things hadn't got off to a bad start. But in the long run, this hermit's life couldn't last. Surviving in winter would be hard. When it started to snow, the police could easily find the camp. Huttunen said that he was thinking of building a hut somewhere deeper in the forest, provided he could settle his money problems first.

'Life in the wilds out here is pretty tough.'

Huttunen said he'd started studying business. He showed Happola the correspondence coursework and used some business terminology. Happola listened attentively.

'If you weren't temporarily, and officially, mad, we'd make a good team. I've never been in business. I'm interested in wholesaling. Why don't you do your course for a start and then we'll see. We could set up a wholesaler's in Oulu or Kemi. I could be on the road visiting clients, and you could take care of the paperwork and everyday stuff.'

Huttunen offered Happola some salted trout. After they'd eaten, he accompanied his friend to the main road. When the men parted company, Happola shook Huttunen's hand for a long time.

'I'll drop you a line over the next couple of days about the purchase of the mill. You'll have the money as soon as the papers are signed, one hundred per cent guaranteed.'

Huttunen returned to his camp extremely satisfied. It had been a long time since he had felt this reassured. The future hadn't seemed so serene for months. He had the prospect of money and he was making progress in his studies ... perhaps he would be able to leave the country with Sanelma Käyrämö soon and start a new life!

CHAPTER 35

Next week, Piittisjärvi made another delivery of mail and vegetables to Sandbank Camp. In her letter, the horticulture adviser Sanelma Käyrämö advised Huttunen not to howl anymore because the governor himself had apparently threatened to send the army to arrest him if he didn't stop his shouting and assaults. She signed off by saying she was desperately in love with Huttunen and stressing the importance of his business studies. She urged him to grate the vegetables Piittisjärvi had brought and have them in a salad.

There was another important letter, from Happola. Huttunen opened it jubilantly, convinced the sale must have gone through. Now he just had to sign the papers and collect the money.

The hermit's disappointment when he read Happola's brief note was brutal. The property developer reported that he couldn't buy the mill because it had been confiscated by the commune's social services unit. Huttunen had been pronounced incapable and was no longer entitled either to sell or mortgage his property.

Under these conditions, the sale is off. Try to get the ban lifted and I'll buy your mill. Look after yourself. Happola

Huttunen seized his rifle and jammed the barrel in his mouth, planning to shoot himself on the spot. Trying to calm his friend, Piittisjärvi said that Huttunen would be mad to kill himself now.

'It would make their day, those fellows in the village.'

Huttunen thought about what the postman was saying; he was right.

'I'm going to burn that bloody mill, then we'll be rid of it!'

He threw his rifle over his shoulder and, without stopping to draw breath, stormed off to the village. Piittisjärvi tried to keep up with him, but he was left behind halfway across Puukko Marsh. The hermit disappeared into the forest. It'll be complete mayhem if Huttunen turns up in the village in that state, Piittisjärvi thought. And with a gun, too . . .

It was afternoon; the hermit's feet sank into the bog at every step, mud spurting out from under them as he ran towards the main road. He charged past the station, rowed across the Kemijoki and tore straight off towards the Suukoski mill, ripping fistfuls of bark from the birch trees he passed. He arrived at the mill drenched in sweat. In a flurry of nails, he wrenched the boards off the front door and raced up to his room.

From the chest by the stove, he took an armful of dry wood, and, hacking at it with a knife, made a pile of twigs. Then he carried both piles downstairs where he made a fire on the floor between the millstones. He propped the logs against each other, put the bark and kindling in the gaps between them, and took his matches out of his pocket. He struck one but he was so agitated and his hands were trembling so badly with rage, it went out.

Huttunen looked round. Everything in the mill was comforting and familiar to him: the walls, the furniture, the hopper, the flour bins. They all seemed to be begging the master of the place for mercy: don't burn us down! Huttunen didn't strike another match. He gathered up the material for the fire, adjusted his rifle on his back and left the mill. He strapped the logs, the kindling and the bark onto the luggage rack of his bicycle, and then he leapt into the saddle, like a light infantryman going off to battle.

'Christ Almighty, I'm going to burn the whole village,' he roared. With his rifle butt knocking against the frame of his bicycle, the hermit pedalled to the centre of the village. Vittavaara's farm, the Siponens' farm, the shop – they all passed. Huttunen slowed down at the shop and thought about setting fire to Tervola's establishment, but decided it was too small a target. His vengeance wouldn't be satisfied with so little. Huttunen didn't stop his bicycle until he got to the fire station. Perhaps he could start there. But then his gaze alighted on the new church, towering over the graveyard, the most imposing monument in the canton, and he had a revelation.

That's what I'm going to burn down to teach them a lesson!

Huttunen cycled through the churchyard to the main door of the church. There was no one about, but the doors were open. He took his things inside and began building a fire in the nave in front of the altar. His rifle butt banged on the ground as he crouched down over the wood, the noise echoing around the big church.

When the fire was ready, Huttunen stood up to dig the matches out of his pocket. He cast a furious, vengeful look around the enormous church. The altarpiece, a painting of Christ on the cross, caught his eye. Huttunen shook his fist at the picture.

'You stupid idiot! Why did you have make me mad?'

The Christ in the altarpiece appeared to look Huttunen straight in the eyes. The Saviour's air of suffering gave way first to an expression of surprise, and then to a look of amused indulgence. He opened his mouth and started speaking. The huge nave echoed as Christ said to the hermit, 'Don't blaspheme, Huttunen. In principle, your mind is no more disturbed than anyone else's. You got good marks in your assignments for the Institute of Education through the Medium of the Post. You're more intelligent than Vittavaara and Siponen put together, and far more so than the pastor of this parish, even though he had the chance to study at university. I've always hated this pastor, he's a completely worthless character, an obnoxious churchman.'

Huttunen listened open-mouthed. Was he going clinically mad, or was the altarpiece talking to him?

Jesus continued in a soft but clear voice.

'Each of us must bear our cross, Huttunen, you just as much as I.'

Huttunen plucked up the courage to contradict Jesus.

'But it's going a bit far in my case! Being hunted like this for six months! I have been freezing in the woods for weeks, and they dragged me off to Oulu asylum ... Couldn't I be spared some of it?'

Jesus nodded understandingly, but then started talking about his own misfortunes.

'Your problems aren't that great, Huttunen, compared to how I was made to suffer.'

Christ's features hardened at the memory of his experiences.

'They persecuted me all my life ... and in the end they nailed me alive to a cross. I've had to suffer, Huttunen. You cannot imagine how painful it is having five-inch copper nails driven through the palms of your hands and the soles of your feet. They forced a crown of thorns on my head and put up the cross. The worst was hanging there, afterwards. No one can understand that pain if they haven't been nailed to a cross themselves.'

Jesus looked seriously at Huttunen.

'I'm a man who has suffered a great deal.'

Huttunen averted his eyes from the altarpiece, and fiddled with his matches. He didn't really know what to say to Jesus.

'But if you've set your heart on burning down this church,' Jesus continued, 'I shan't object. I've never liked this building much. I prefer the old church on the hill. It was megalomania that made them build this. But don't light your fire right in front of the altar. Go into the sacristy or the vestibule, the fire will spread better from there; the church is dry. And could you take away that rifle? It's not very appropriate coming in here with your arms full of logs and a rifle on your back. You are in a consecrated place, after all.'

Faintly embarrassed, Huttunen knelt down before the image of Christ, gathered up his wood from in front of the altar and took it into the vestibule. There, he quickly lit the fire. The twigs and bark merrily burst into flames. Thick smoke filled the vestibule and the nave.

The entrance was soon so obscured that Huttunen had to open the door of the church, and retreat to the nave where he sat on a pew, rubbing his eyes. He'd never have thought such a small fire could produce so much smoke; it must have been because there was no breeze.

A cloud of smoke escaped through the open door, floated over the graveyard and drifted off towards the village past the firemen's tower. The first firemen came running, buckets rattling in their hands. Huttunen, mean-while, was trying to stir up the fire in the vestibule. He blew on the embers, setting them glowing; new flames leapt up. The smoke kept on forcing him back into the nave.

Outside, he could hear the people who'd come to put out the fire shouting. The pall of smoke in the church grew even denser as they began throwing water on the fire. The blaze hissed; the flames shrank back. Huttunen couldn't see the firemen, but judging by the voices, there were a lot of them. He had to get away; he wouldn't be able to get the better of such a crowd. Taking a deep breath, Huttunen ran into the church vestibule, jumped over the spitting embers and out into the open air, his gun on his back, his hands clamped over his streaming eyes. The stunned onlookers parted before him. Soon he could see clearly enough to hurtle across the churchyard. He jumped over the graves, leapt the hedge and disappeared into the forest.

Police Chief Jaatila arrived at the scene. He established the fire was out. When he was told the hermit Gunnar Huttunen had tried to burn down the church, he said in a tone that brooked no argument, 'Starting tomorrow morning, we are going to organise a massive manhunt. I'm going to ring Rovaniemi to get them to send us soldiers and army dogs.'

CHAPTER 36

One morning, a goods train, a rare sight in those parts, stopped at the station. At the rear of the train there was a cattle truck, which opened its double doors to reveal half a section of helmeted light infantry – bicycle-mounted division – who promptly leapt out onto the platform. They had an army tent, a field kitchen and two army dogs in tow, and each of the men was armed with a machine pistol. On the sergeants' bellowed orders, the detachment fell into line. The commanding officer, a tough young lieutenant, presented his men to Police Chief Jaatila.

'Welcome, soldiers!' Jaatila said. 'A dangerous and difficult mission awaits you, but I have every confidence in you and especially your dogs.'

The police chief offered the lieutenant a cigarette. The sergeants drew the men up in marching order; the detachment noisily set off towards the ferry. Vittavaara's horse was hitched to the field kitchen. The army dogs and the lieutenant got into the police chief's car. The dogs were muzzled for safety's sake; they were big Alsatians with thick coats, sinister, nervy-looking creatures. The lieutenant stroked one and proudly told the police chief, 'This one's Terror of the Frontiers, that one's White Nose. No sense of humour, these two.'

Disembarking from the ferry, the soldiers headed towards the sports ground where a crowd of civilians with rifles and rucksacks was gathered. Including the women and children, there were more people than there had been spectators at the provincial athletics championships.

Equipped with a loudspeaker, the police chief gave orders. Provisions and maps were distributed. The farmers were divided into groups of ten. The sun was shining, ideal weather to start a major operation. The farmers were supplied with cartridges; the border guards loaded their machine pistols.

'This could be tough going,' one of the infantrymen said.

'I prefer a manhunt to a forest fire,' his companion replied. 'Last summer we spent two whole weeks putting one out in Narkaus. By the end all of us had a layer of soot on our faces an inch deep.'

'In the war, I was sent after two or three enemy spies who'd parachuted in behind our lines. Hunting this nutter should be the same sort of job.'

'Lucky they've given us helmets,' said another soldier.

'Apparently he's got a rifle. Unless he gets a clean shot, it'll ricochet off.'

The lieutenant ordered the men to be quiet and listen to the police chief's instructions. Jaatila was winding up his talk.

'So once again I want to emphasise that the man we are hunting is armed and extremely dangerous. If he doesn't give himself up at the first command, force will have to be resorted to. I'm sure I make myself quite clear.'

The police chief turned to the lieutenant.

'Between you and me . . . With this Huttunen, you can shoot on sight.'

'I understand.'

The search party was split in two: twenty-odd civilians were detailed to comb the forest east of the Kemijoki while the bulk of the men took the ferry back across the river to search the woods to the west. The police chief set up his command post at the station.

When the postman Piittisjärvi heard of these developments, he instantly feared for his still. He leapt on his bicycle, overtook the soldiers and pedalled to Huttunen's letterbox, where he hid his bike and dashed off at top speed to save his moonshine and warn Huttunen in the process. Sandbank Camp was deserted. He called Huttunen quietly, but got no answer. He guessed the hermit had gone fishing on the river, since his rifle and tackle were nowhere to be seen.

Piittisjärvi dismantled his still, hid the vats and pipes among the roots of some tall black firs and pulled his

ARTO PAASILINNA

churn of firewater out of the waterhole. It still contained at least eight pints of wildwood's tears.

Piittisjärvi left a note on Huttunen's rucksack.

Huttunen, the army is on your tail. Take to your heels.
Piittisjärvi

The postman hoisted the churn of hooch onto his back and left the camp. His plan was to get back to the safety of the main road before the troops could search the area. But he had to act quickly; no time for a cigarette. He barely even dared take the odd sip from his churn.

This was the second time Piittisjärvi had been forced to evacuate his set-up that summer. He may have had to hurry the first time, but this was a real emergency. He pelted across the shifting bog and through the dense brush with just one thought in mind: to get across the road before the forest was crawling with the soldiers.

But the well-trained border guards had quickly fanned out and were silently moving through the trees in a long line. Dripping with sweat, the little postman was easy pickings. One of the dogs let out a brief howl and would have torn him to pieces if its handler hadn't come to his rescue with its muzzle.

Piittisjärvi and his moonshine were taken to the police chief's command post at the station. Jaatila questioned the postman briefly and then Portimo took him to the cells. The grog was pitilessly poured out onto the ground. Tears welled in the postman's eyes.

In the afternoon, the infantrymen found Huttunen's camp, destroyed it and took the message left by Piittisjärvi to the police chief. Jaatila immediately ran to his cell and gave the postman a tremendous thrashing with his lead-filled truncheon. Piittisjärvi wept and moaned and begged in vain for mercy. The police chief demanded information about Huttunen but the fellow refused to give him anything. The hermit's post was produced – the assignments set by the Institute of Education through the Medium of the Post, a few love letters, the last communication from Happola. How had Huttunen got his post? Covered in bruises, Piittisjärvi was heroic.

'You can kill me, but I'll never betray a friend.'

Nor did he, despite receiving another beating from the police chief. When Jaatila stormed out of his cell in a fury, Piittisjärvi shouted after him, 'I'll never divulge postal secrets to a cur like you!'

The police chief called in Sanelma Käyrämö and subjected her to intense questioning. But the adviser didn't admit anything, despite being threatened with the wrath of the provincial governor and the entire 4H Federation. Sanelma Käyrämö burst into floods of tears and begged Jaatila to be lenient towards Huttunen, saying that if he could just put his side of events, she was sure he'd leave the woods of his own free will. The police chief took due note of this, and then, with utter disdain, spat, 'Do you want me to tell you what I think of women who molly-coddle lunatics? They're worse than whores!'

The dogs were turned loose on Sandbank Camp.

Wagging their tails, they dashed off in pursuit of the hermit, leading the soldiers upstream along the Puukko. Huttunen's trail was fresh, and the excited Alsatians raced through the undergrowth on the bank, whimpering and barking with complete disregard for their handlers' injunctions to be quiet.

Huttunen was fly-fishing on the banks of the Puukko, at the edge of a peat bog. He had already caught a couple of grayling and was thinking of going back to his camp. He lit a cigarette and gazed in a melancholy way at the slow-moving stream. The light was going. Huttunen wanted to write to Sanelma Käyrämö and tell her the latest news. Now that he wouldn't be able to sell the mill, perhaps he should go further north and build a cabin deep in the forest where he could spend the winter. He needed to split a pair of skis, make a few barrels, pick berries and shoot a brace of game birds. Perhaps it would be good to smoke an elk for the winter. The hermit's keen hearing picked up the sound of barking somewhere downstream. Straining his ears, Huttunen could make out men's muffled voices. Raising his binoculars to his eyes, he scanned the marsh on the opposite bank. In the gathering twilight, he saw helmeted soldiers in grey uniforms. Two big hounds were racing along the stream in his direction. The hermit instantly guessed they were after him. He loaded his rifle, abandoned his fishing tackle and his catch on the bank and fled as he fast he could towards a little hill on the other side of the marsh.

The dogs soon reached the deserted fishing spot. They

threw themselves on the fish lying on the ground, tearing them to pieces. Huttunen lined up one of the dogs in his sights and fired. It gave a little yelp, and then keeled over dead. The second dog came bounding across the marsh towards the hill where Huttunen was lying on his stomach, the rifle pressed to his cheek. When the animal was only fifty feet away, Huttunen fired again. It somersaulted into the air, then fell back on its side without a noise. The border guards formed ranks and stormed the hill, one of them firing a brief burst of machine-gun fire.

Huttunen fled north. He ran as fast as he could.

You're going to have to be strapping lads if you're going to take me alive.

All night the light infantrymen swept the forest without catching a glimpse of Huttunen. In the early hours of the morning, they regrouped at Sandbank Camp, where Vittavaara had taken the field kitchen on a sledge. The army tent was pitched, and the exhausted farmers and soldiers congregated to eat and sleep.

The dead dogs were hung from a pole by their paws. Four men were detailed to take them to the village. When the exhausted party arrived at the police chief's command post, he pointed at the dogs and sneered, 'Have you brought these carcasses back to lay them in consecrated ground?'

'Don't push your luck!' the lieutenant bristled. 'At least we found the lunatic's camp.'

The lieutenant gave orders for the dogs to be buried. The infantry dug them a grave at the station crossroads, next to the transformer. Father Rasti's farm nearby was holding a prayer meeting that evening. A hymn rehearsal could be heard in the distance. The lieutenant cursed, 'Get a move on and bury those dogs. They're singing psalms now, for God's sake. What sort of yokel town is this?'

In the farm, the lay preacher Leskelä was testifying and praying for Huttunen.

'Dear Sweet Lord, receive the former miller Huttunen into your care with all due haste, or else deliver him forthwith into the hands of the army, in the name of the body and blood of Jesus Christ, Amen.'

CHAPTER 37

For three days the soldiers and the canton's male popu-
lation combed the woods and bogs in vain. Then the
farmers discreetly went home, hung up their guns and
returned to work in the fields. The border guards packed
up their tent, took the field kitchen back to the station
and loaded their kit into the cattle truck. Without further
ado, this was coupled to a goods train heading north. The
steam locomotive whistled, and then the army was gone.

The only legacy of the great manhunt was a mound
slowly being overgrown at the station crossroads. Under
the earth lay two heroic army dogs. The little children
developed a habit that autumn of coming every Sunday
and singing on their grave the same hymns of Zion that
the preacher Leskelä led them through at prayer meetings.

Once a day, Police Chief Jaatila went to the cells to
give the postman Piittisjärvi a thrashing, but it was a waste

of energy. Tough as boots, the man heroically endured the blows in the name of the inviolability of postal secrecy.

Since neither force nor numbers had enabled him to catch Huttunen, the police chief resolved to use cunning. He paid a visit to the horticultural adviser Sanelma Käyrämö and told her that the authorities had finally decided to let the hermit off. He still had to make the first move, however, and come out of the woods.

'Let's go to the jail and tell Piittisjärvi that he can take Huttunen an official letter of amnesty. Your hermit's misdemeanours will be forgotten, I swear. We'll just give him a small fine, that's all.'

The police chief wrote Huttunen a letter. The adviser added a little note asking him to come to the village and give himself up. The past would be forgiven.

The police chief took the letters and went with the adviser to convince the postman to deliver them.

Piittisjärvi initially suspected a trap, but when the police chief stamped on the letter of reprieve with the official police stamp and sealed it with wax, the postman thought justice had triumphed and promised to take the message to Huttunen. But only if he could do it alone, with no one knowing where he would be going.

The police chief readily agreed. A vast plate of steaming pork hotpot was immediately brought to Piittisjärvi's cell. He was given a packet of Saimaa cigarettes and after the meal, the village masseur, Asikainen, came and rubbed liniment into the patchwork of black bruises on his back, souvenirs of the police chief's lead-filled truncheon. At dusk, the cell door opened and Piittisjärvi was let out to do the job he'd been given.

The police chief had organised the tailing cleverly: he, the farmhand Launola and Vittavaara followed the postman to the station and slipped through the woods as the old fellow made his way to Huttunen's letterbox. Piittisjärvi kept looking behind him, checking to see he was alone, but even so he didn't notice anyone following him. He went ahead, therefore, and took the letters to their destination, and then casually returned to the road.

As soon as Piittisjärvi had revealed the letterbox's whereabouts, he was picked up, and unceremoniously returned to his cell. His protests were futile, but he did at least escape a beating this time, because the chief was in a hurry to get into position.

Jaatila and the villagers kept watch on the letterbox for a day and a half before the trap could snap shut. The starving Huttunen finally appeared around five in the morning to check the contents of his letterbox. The farm-hand Launola, who was on guard, immediately ran to tell the police chief.

Huttunen approached the letterbox warily but, once he was convinced the forest was empty, he was emboldened to take a look. He read the police chief's and adviser's letters several times. When he understood what a fantastic offer they contained, all his anxiety vanished and, although he was exhausted, he could feel renewed hope and strength coursing through his veins. And so the trap had been sprung. Now the hunters lying in wait could strike.

Huttunen jammed the letters in his pocket and went to the crossroads. He took the ferry road, but he had barely time to go any distance before his trackers jumped him from both sides of the road. Taken totally by surprise, he was thrown to the ground and his hands and feet bound in a flash. The chief thwacked him across the back a few times with his truncheon so hard his shoulder blades rattled. Vittavaara brought up his horse and cart, and in no time the road was echoing to the old gelding's hooves as it galloped towards the ferry.

Huttunen lay trussed up with the chief and Vittavaara sitting on top of him, lashing the horse. When they reached the landing stage, the gelding was steaming and foaming from having been ridden so hard. Silent and unmoving on the floor of the cart, Huttunen lay staring sadly at the sky.

News of the hermit's capture had reached the village on the other side of the river. When the ferry berthed, a tightly packed crowd was waiting. Relieved and delighted in equal measure, the locals stared at the prize in the cart. They asked Huttunen if he still wanted to howl. Was he thinking of ringing the bells? Had he come to set fire to the church or rob the bank again, with a horse this time?

The schoolteacher Tanhumäki had brought his camera. The gelding was stopped for a picture. The teacher made his way through the crowd and asked Jaatila to take the reins so he could get a shot of the horse, the police chief, the cart and, in the background, its cargo. Huttunen turned his face away but Launola wrenched his head round. Huttunen shut his eyes as the shutter clicked. When the photo had been taken, the police chief handed the reins back to Vittavaara who lashed the horse's crupper.

The hermit was driven to the station. The police chief ordered Constable Portimo to come into the cell with them. Huttunen was seated on the concrete bench next to Portimo. The police chief handcuffed the police constable's left wrist to the hermit's right. He only undid the prisoner's hands and feet after that, and then went out of the cell, leaving Portimo and Huttunen sitting hand in hand. Jaatila looked through the peephole in the door and said to the police constable, 'You stay there and look after that lunatic.'

The flap banged shut; the police chief's footsteps receded down the corridor.

Portimo and Huttunen were left on their own. The constable said sadly, 'So here you are, Kunnari.'

'Accidents happen,' Huttunen replied.

Next morning the police chief had the prisoner and his guard brought to his office. Siponen, Vittavaara and Ervinen were present. Jaatila handed Portimo a letter written by Ervinen, addressed to Oulu mental hospital. The police chief also gave the police constable travel vouchers for the train. Taking them, Portimo couldn't help remarking, 'Even a police chief should keep his word. It's not fair sending Kunnari back to Oulu.'

'Oh be quiet! The police aren't bound by promises they make to the insane. Just keep your mouth shut and do your job, Portimo. The train leaves at eleven; we'll give Huttunen something to eat first. You'll both travel in the

ticket inspector's compartment. This man is your responsibility, Portimo.'

Ervinen gave Huttunen an ironic look.

'It's been a long summer, and a lot of fun, Huttunen,
but it's over now. Speaking as a doctor, I can assure you
that you will never have another chance to come and
play the fool in this canton. That letter says that you are
afflicted by an incurable mental illness, and will remain
so for the rest of your life. You've howled your last howl,
Huttunen.'

Huttunen suddenly started growling and baring his
teeth. He ducked his head and flattened his ears in such
a menacing way that the farmers and doctor backed away
and the police chief took his pistol out of his desk drawer.
A dull moaning rose from the hermit's throat, his teeth
glinted. With great difficulty, Portimo gradually managed
to calm his friend. Huttunen continued growling for a
long time like a wolf trapped in its lair, his eyes flashing
with suppressed fury.

The hermit and police constable were driven by car to
Portimo's house, where Huttunen was given a last meal.
Portimo's wife had grilled some fish. She put fresh buttermilk, piping hot barley bread and good butter on the
table. For dessert, there were pancakes. Huttunen and
Portimo ate side by side, one with his left hand, the other
with his right. The police chief impatiently observed the
meal's progress.

'Come on, eat up. What on earth gave you the idea of
making pancakes for a mad prisoner? You really didn't

need to go to so much trouble. They mustn't miss the train. We've got to resolve this as soon as possible.'

The horticultural adviser Sanelma Käyrämö came in. She had been crying all night. She went up to Huttunen without a word and put her hand on his shoulder. Turning towards the police chief, she said in a broken voice, 'And I believed this traitor, fool that I am.'

Embarrassed, the police chief coughed officiously, and then resumed chivvying the men. Portimo and Huttunen got up from the table. Huttunen clasped Sanelma's hand in his left hand, looked into her eyes and then followed Portimo out.

Outside the police constable said goodbye to his wife. Then he led Huttunen to the shed, whistling for his dog. The grey spitz ran barking towards his master, jumped up and licked his face. He gave Huttunen, who had been forced to bend down by the handcuffs, a good lick as well.

'For Christ's sake, now they're saying goodbye to their dogs,' the police chief grunted impatiently.

Portimo and Huttunen were put in the car, the doors slammed and they set off for the ferry, where the fastest cyclists had already congregated. A dense throng waited at the station. The whole canton wanted to see Huttunen board the train for his last journey to Oulu.

The police chief asked the stationmaster if the train was on time and was told it should be.

'Why isn't it here then?' Jaatila exploded.

'Some trains are not as on time as others,' the stationmaster replied.

The train pulled into the station. The heavy steam locomotive came to a halt. Huttunen and Portimo were
escorted along the platform to the ticket inspector's
compartment. They stepped simultaneously into the
carriage. The train whistled and began moving. Huttunen
stood at the open door, the silhouette of Constable Portimo
visible behind him. The train passed before the crowd on
the platform. Huttunen opened his mouth, and a tremendous howl rose into the air. Alongside it, the train's whistle
seemed like a feeble chirping. The carriage left the horrified spectators behind. The door closed. The shunt
screeched on the edge of the rails; the train pulled away
into the distance. It was only when the noise of its wheels
had completely died away that the crowd started to break
up. Constable Portimo's wife left the station apart from
the others, supported by the horticultural adviser Sanelma
Käyrämö, in tears. The police chief got in his car and
drove off. The stationmaster rolled up his green flag,
muttering, 'That was a bigger turnout than for the
governor.'

CHAPTER 38

Word soon got out that Huttunen and Portimo had failed to reach Oulu mental hospital. Police Chief Jaatila circulated their particulars throughout the country, but no information was forthcoming about what had happened to the two men. Not even Interpol could find out any details of their whereabouts.

That autumn, the horticulture adviser Sanelma Käyrämö moved in with Constable Portimo's wife as a lodger. They ate their meals together, which, by and large, were pretty decent ones, thanks to their economical love of vegetables. Piittisjärvi, who had time on his hands since losing his job as postman, took care of all the heavy lifting.

In October, Portimo's grey spitz ran off . . . It disappeared into the forest. When winter came, its tracks were found in the Reutu marshes. It didn't roam the woods alone but accompanied a big wolf, a lone male judging by the tracks. On nights when there was a heavy frost, the wolf's plaintive howling could be heard in the marshes, sometimes accompanied by the melancholy barking of Portimo's dog.

It was said in the village that the wolf and dog often came prowling round the houses at night. People claimed the horticulture adviser and the constable's wife fed them secretly.

Shortly before Christmas, the two animals were found to have got into Siponen's hen coop. All twenty of his chickens had their throats torn open.

When Vittaavara killed the pig he'd been fattening up for Christmas in Advent week and hung it, scalded and scraped, from a beam in his barn, it vanished overnight. The fresh tracks of a dog and wolf were found on the ground. The pig was never recovered.

During the winter, these shaggy beasts surprised Police Chief Jaatila and Dr Ervinen out on the ice of Reutu pond. The men were fishing at a hole when the dog and the wolf burst out of the forest and fell on them. The men would have been dead meat if they hadn't managed to climb the pines at the edge of the pond. Growling savagely, the wolf and dog kept the police chief and doctor prisoner for thirty-six hours. The animals ate the food in their backpacks and nudged their thermoses through the hole in the ice into the water. The police chief's right arm was frozen to the elbow, as was the doctor's nose. They would have died in their frost-covered pines if a sympathetic lumberjack had not come to their rescue.

Mrs Siponen had acquired the habit of going to church every Sunday. Since she still claimed to be disabled, the hired man Launola had to harness the horse each time. The farmwife was carried straight from the sleigh to her pew in the church, where she sprawled out. She took up as much room in the front row as five parishioners, but everyone was happy to oblige the poor woman who couldn't move a muscle.

One day, a raw-boned wolf and a tousled spitz attacked the horse and sleigh on the frozen Kemijoki on its way to church. The horse shied and broke its shafts, the sleigh tipped over, the hired man fled on the gelding, and the corpulent Mrs Siponen was left spread-eagled on the ice at the mercy of her attackers. She wouldn't have survived if she hadn't run for it on her short legs and taken refuge in the ferryman's house. The tracks of the poor paralysed woman's flight across the frozen Kemijoki excited unanimous admiration, especially among athletics fans.

The local men tried every way imaginable to kill the wolf and dog, but they could never catch them. They were too cunning and daring, and, what's more, utterly inseparable. Together, they made a savage, terrifying pair. On icy nights, when the wolf's heart-rending howls could be heard coming from Mount Reutu, people would say, 'In a way, Huttunen's howling sounded more natural.'

TRANSLATOR'S NOTE

This novel begins 'Soon after the wars', that is to say, shortly after the Second World War, which was marked in Finland by two wars against the USSR.

In November 1939, when Finland refused to grant the USSR strategic bases for its defence of Kronstadt and Leningrad, the Soviets bombed Helsinki. This was the start of the 'Winter War', which lasted one hundred and five days and resulted in heavy losses on both sides. Despite courageous resistance north of Lake Ladoga and along the Oulu–Suomussalmi line, Finland was compelled by the Treaty of Moscow to cede part of Karelia and Lapland to the Soviet Union.

In June 1941, after allowing the transit of supplies to German troops in Norway, Finland was led to agree to cooperate militarily with the Third Reich against the USSR. It thereby embarked on the 'War of Continuation' and fought to regain its lost territory until the withdrawal of the Wehrmacht in August 1944, which left the Ladoga front exposed and drove Finland to open peace negotiations. Finland signed an armistice with the USSR, which required it to pay substantial reparations, return to the borders of 1940 and break off relations with Germany.

The Finnish troops then turned on the German units stationed in Lapland, which systematically devastated the region during their retreat; fighting continued there until April 1945.

Anne Colin du Terrail, 1991